Remembering Mrs. Rossi

Remembering Mrs. Rossi

AMY HEST

illustrated by
Heather Maione

CANDLEWICK PRESS
CAMBRIDGE, MASSACHUSETTS

For my mother
A. H.

Text copyright © 2007 by Amy Hest
Illustrations copyright © 2007 by Heather Maione

First edition 2007

Library of Congress Cataloging-in-Publication Data
Hest, Amy
Remembering Mrs. Rossi / Amy Hest ; illustrated by Heather Maione. — 1st ed.
p.   cm.
Summary: Although she loves her father, their home in New York City, and
third-grade teacher Miss Meadows, Annie misses her mother who died recently.
ISBN 978-0-7636-2163-6
[1. Death — Fiction. 2. Parent and child — Fiction. 3. New York (N.Y.) — Fiction.]
I. Maione, Heather Harms, ill. II. Title.
PZ7.H4375Re 2007
[Fic] — dc22   2006041649

2 4 6 8 10 9 7 5 3 1

Printed in the United States of America

This book was typeset in Kennerley.
The illustrations were done in ink with black watercolor wash.

Candlewick Press
2067 Massachusetts Avenue
Cambridge, Massachusetts 02140

visit us at www.candlewick.com

Contents

MEETING ANNIE ROSSI, AGE 8

*O*nce upon a time in New York City, there was a tall brick building on a wide winding street called Riverside Drive.

Forty-five families lived there in forty-five apartments on fifteen floors. They had a flower garden on the roof, and in the basement, a bright yellow room with six washing machines. The elevator was noisy and slow, but the lobby was grand—cool white marble and that big marble staircase in the middle. All in all, it was a fine apartment house, and if you were lucky enough to live there, you had your very own park right across the street.

In that building, at that time, was a family called Rossi.

Their house was on the tenth floor—apartment 10B—and sunlight filled the rooms. Sometimes at night the moon showed up, just like that, and they stood at the windows watching the moon. And stars. And boats on the Hudson River. The front door was red. The living room was also painted red, and everywhere you looked were family photos. And books, the place was bursting with books.

Mrs. Rossi knew a lot about books. Especially sixth-grade books. And fifth-grade books. Mrs. Rossi was a sixth-grade teacher, and some years a fifth-grade teacher, at the Louis Armstrong School. She had soft green eyes and dark wavy hair, and she was always dashing off to the New York Public Library, hauling books back and forth in her wagon.

Professor Rossi was a teacher, too, at Columbia University, a very big school that was just up the hill, a five-minute walk to Broadway. Professor

Rossi had curly hair and extra-long feet, and he read all the time. All kinds of books, including a great many fat ones with tiny little print.

Annie Rossi liked books about girls, and now that she was eight, she especially liked books about girls who were eight. She also liked books about dogs. Annie had dark brown eyes, short brown hair, and a tiny scar on her chin. She loved her scar very much and looked at it often in the privacy of the bathroom. Also, she loved telling the story of her scar. It always began: Once upon a time when I was little. It always ended: And that is the story of my scar. In between, there was a very big drama about a new green bike, a too-big hill, a trip to the emergency room, and chocolate ice cream.

Each year when summer came, the Rossis took a place at the beach—45 Pineapple Street—a three-room cottage steps from the sea.

The porch had a hammock and the screen door

creaked and they dined at a picnic table. Summer-time! The Rossis ran on the beach and swam in the sea, and they were always taking pictures. They walked into town quite often. The town had one little street called Main Street with a big old library right in the middle. Annie played with the neighbor girl, Helen, nearly every day. (Helen was okay, but her dog, Al, was really fun!)

But sooner or later, all summers end. That year—like every year—the family bid goodbye to the beach and the neighbors and Al, and took the slow train home. It was time to get ready for school. There were lessons to plan and first-day-of-school clothes to plan, new notebooks and pencils and shoes. When the first day came, they all had a case of the jitters. But the next day was better, and the day after that. A week slipped by, and then one more. Shoes got scuffed, notebooks messy. The days were shorter now and cool. The Rossis went out into the world each morning, each to a different school, and came together again at night. They were always swapping stories.

One morning Mrs. Rossi did not go to school. (Mommy's not feeling well, Annie.) Her fever soared, then dipped, and soared again. (Dr. Warren is coming to see what's up with Mommy, Annie.) Everyone talked in strange whispers. (Pneumonia, they whispered, and hospital.) Annie tried to be brave. The girls in her library books always seemed to have a great deal of courage, and she wanted to be a girl with courage, too. So she told herself — quite sternly — No crying in front of Mommy! But no matter how hard she tried, it was impossible not to cry when your mother was in the hospital. "Mommy, come home now," Annie whispered, "and I'll be your nurse and we'll watch TV on the couch and then you'll be all better. . . ."

The leaves in the park were especially gold that fall. Everyone spoke of the leaves. And the skies were especially blue. Everyone spoke of the bright blue skies . . . and nobody, absolutely nobody, expected Mrs. Rossi to die.

ONE

The Night Walks

It is a cold winter night, but eight-year-old Annie Rossi is out on the town with her father.

"I'm *freeeezing*, Daddy!" Annie skips into the wind. "Are you freezing, too?"

"Definitely. Should we hop on a bus to warm up?"

"Definitely not," Annie says.

"Taxi?"

Annie shakes her head.

"Subway, then?"

"Daddy, did you forget?" She reaches for his hand. "It's a night *walk*."

The night walks. Not every night, of course. Just when the house is too big and too quiet and Annie is waiting forever for sleep. Sometimes she tells herself wonderful secrets while she waits. *Oh, Mommy's just inside. She's reading on the couch in her fuzzy blue robe as usual, eating coffee ice cream on the couch as usual, in her little green bowl. . . .* And some nights the door opens a crack and her father peeks in. Annie pretends to sleep. She likes watching him cross the room to the big chair near the window. She likes watching him watch the moon.

On the night of the first walk, Annie remembers, there was no moon. . . .

✽

"Hello," she had whispered from her bed that night.

"Hello," he whispered back.

"Are you reading your book over there?" Annie sat up. "I like when you read in my room at night."

"To be honest, I'm not in the mood for this book right now."

"Is it scary? Don't worry, Daddy. Sometimes I'm not in the mood for scary stories, either." Annie sighed sympathetically. In the next breath, though, she got a great idea. A milk-and-cookie idea. "I *bet* you're in the mood for a snack," she said. "If you want, I could keep you company. . . ."

Annie slipped out of bed, and they went to the kitchen and sat on the counter awhile, dipping cookies in milk. They didn't talk much, but it was terribly exciting to be eating cookies in the night, and at ten that night Annie still wasn't tired. So they played gin rummy, and—for the first time ever—she won three games in a row! Understandably, all that winning left her much too giggly for sleep. So they watched TV on the couch and looked at the pictures in old magazines. Ten thirty came . . . and soon it was 10:50 . . . and Annie was still full of pep. Still wide awake!

"I'm wide awake," she announced.

Professor Rossi yawned a big noisy yawn.

"So, Daddy, what should we do now? More TV?"

But Professor Rossi had something else in mind. "Something *unconventional*," he promised on his way to the closet for coats. (His was long and brown; Annie's short and blue.)

"Okay!" he called.

"Okay what, Daddy?"

"Okay, we're going out."

"Now?" Annie's nose wrinkled up with excitement. "In the middle of the *night?*"

Annie buttoned her coat right over pajamas. Then they walked up the hill to Broadway, and Professor Rossi told some things about her baby days. "Hmmm . . . now let me think . . ." he began. "I seem to remember . . . you were a fairly bald but cheery baby. Very pleasant, Annie. Except, of course, you hated going to sleep. Oh, the tears and commotion!"—shaking his head— "Only one thing worked."

"What thing?"

"A little night walk. We bundled you into your carriage for a little night walk."

"Mommy, too?" Annie whispered.

"Of course, Mommy, too."

"Who pushed the carriage?"

"Mommy. Mostly Mommy, but don't you worry . . . I did my share."

"And *I* stopped crying."

"Mm-hmm." Professor Rossi nodded. "Our little scheme worked like a charm," he told Annie. "As a matter of fact, by the time we hit this very spot on Broadway, you were sleepy and calm."

"And Mommy said, 'What a great little *perfect* baby! What an *angel!*'" Annie crooned. "Then what, Daddy?"

"Then, in honor of the fact that you were *finally* asleep"—joking—"we took ourselves to Carmen's Diner and ordered up a really good treat."

"What kind of treat? What was Mommy's favorite?"

"Pancakes, definitely. And we sat in a booth with turquoise seats, and Mommy played with your tiny fingers, Annie, while you slept in the carriage beside her."

Yes, Annie loved to hear some things about her baby days. She especially loved the parts about her mother.

Tonight, of course, Annie wouldn't *think* of wearing pajamas underneath her coat. Because on this night walk, they are going to the Louis Armstrong School—her mother's school—for a special assembly. Annie is all dressed up for the occasion. She is wearing her favorite red dress and her shoes are brand-new. Terribly fancy, too, with a strap across the middle. They make a fine clicking sound on pavement. One, two, *click!* Can't be *late!* One, two, *click!* Can't be *late!*

The invitation had come in the mail, and Annie knew every word by heart.

```
Dear Professor Rossi and Annie,

You are cordially invited to Winter
Assembly. Thursday night at 7:00.
Offerings by the Glee Club and
Orchestra. Plus a Beautiful Surprise!!

We look forward to seeing you both.

Very truly yours,
Vera Owens, principal
```

And now it is seven o'clock. It is Thursday night, and the Louis Armstrong School is all lit up, bright lights glowing in every window, upstairs and down. The front doors are wide open, a banner tacked overhead: WELCOME TO WINTER ASSEMBLY. Yes, it is seven o'clock. It is

Thursday night, and Annie Rossi stands across the street from her mother's school. And somewhere in that school, upstairs on two, is her mother's classroom. Annie stands there in new shoes and her favorite dress, watching kids of all ages and grownups scramble inside to the All-Purpose Room. Annie squeezes her eyes tight. Perhaps if she squeezes them very tight, she'll see her mother there, too, in her long red coat. . . .

Annie shuffles her feet, looking down at her shoes and her white summer socks. Short *ankle* socks instead of cozy *winter* socks, and whose fault is that! Annie glances sideways at her father and frowns. Why, it's *his* fault she's cold, because *he* forgot to say, "Wear warm socks, Annie—knee socks so your legs don't freeze. . . ."

"Maybe we shouldn't be here." Professor

Rossi's voice is far away. "It's too hard being here without Mommy."

"I *like* being here! I want to go to Winter Assembly!" Annie certainly doesn't mean to stamp her foot three times in a row like some awful little child in a temper. Nor does she mean to shout. But sometimes you just can't help it, and there you are stamping away and shouting at your father—and you don't know why.

Annie's thoughts turn to another time, another temper. This one on the day before the first day of third grade, and she is shopping for new school shoes with her mother. Annie likes the shiny red ones with red velvet bows. "I ONLY want these, Mommy, and I'll ONLY get these!" But Mrs. Rossi, the boss of school shoes, has other ideas—plain old *brown* ideas—and in spite of Annie's stamping (or perhaps *because* of her stamping), she winds up with the plain old browns that day. The shoes make her mad! "No one in third grade wears ugly brown shoes!" And her mother is mean! "Now everyone will say, 'Let's not be friends with Annie Rossi . . .' and it's all YOUR fault . . . and I WISH you weren't my mother. . . ."

Annie shudders in the cold night air. Why, why, *why* had she said all those bad things to her mother that time? Maybe she *is* just an awful little child . . . and who in the world would want *her* for a child? Absolutely no one! Not even her own mother, and perhaps that's why she doesn't have a mother anymore. *Mommy, come back . . . and I'll be good every second, and perfect. . . .* Suddenly, Annie starts to cry. She doesn't mean to, of course. Not here, not tonight. But sometimes you just can't help it.

Professor Rossi and Annie sit on a stoop, and they both watch the school. It is dark on the stoop, and chilly, and they sit very close, hugging their knees and each other, and Annie slowly calms down. Every now and then, she looks up at the sky, wishing for snow. Wishing she could make a snowman with her mother in the park. Just one more time. One more snowman with a silly carrot nose. Inside the Louis Armstrong School, the glee club sings. The orchestra plays.

"I miss Mommy," Annie tells her father in between sniffles.

"And I miss Mommy," he says, blowing his nose.

"But I miss her more," Annie insists. "Nobody misses her more than me."

A few minutes later, they cross the street.

They walk under the banner and into the school and find two empty seats in the very last row of the All-Purpose Room. At the very front of the room, Mrs. Owens, the principal, is holding two fingers in the air for silence. "And now"—she smiles broadly as the audience settles down— "for the final event of the evening, one of our sixth-grade classes will make a special presentation. It's all about memories of someone they—and we—have loved very much. Ladies and gentlemen, boys and girls . . . I give you . . . room 222!"

The curtain goes up. Behind Mrs. Owens, the kids from room 222 (there are twenty-four in all) make a jittery and solemn line across the stage. You could hear a pin drop in the All-Purpose Room.

A girl steps out of line, taking two steps

forward. She has short hair and it is very black, and her dress is very pink. She holds a book in both hands and leans toward the microphone. "My name is Julie," she begins in a shaky voice. "The whole class took a vote and we voted for me, and that's why I get to talk at Winter Assembly. I'm supposed to start with Mr. Shaw. That's our sub and he's pretty nice. Most of the time. But we still call ourselves Mrs. Rossi's class, no offense, Mr. Shaw. We were lucky. Because we got to have Mrs. Rossi *two* years in a row. Fifth *and* sixth grade.

"I'm also supposed to say it was Mr. Shaw who thought up the idea to make a book about our teacher . . . but if you want to know who did all the work," Julie boasts, "*we* did. That's right, the *kids* are the authors!

"Boy, were there fights," she goes on.

"*Thousands!* No one could agree on one little thing, including what the title should be. We have a good one, though: **Remembering Mrs. Rossi** . . . and it's all about Mrs. Rossi . . . and you can't believe how great it is, no kidding!

"We have big hearts, too. Because after all that hard work, we're not even keeping our book. *We're giving it away!*" Julie sucks in her breath. "Okay, to tell you the truth, no one *wanted* to give it away. Unless you count Mr. Shaw. He thought giving it away was a 'beautiful gesture.' He kept saying, 'Who do you think would most appreciate having a book called **Remembering Mrs. Rossi**?' Then Matthew called out, 'Mrs. Rossi's family! I bet they'd appreciate it!' Which was definitely the right answer, because after that Mr. Shaw was in a good mood nine days in a row."

Mrs. Owens is clapping now, and dabbing her eyes with a hankie. She calls across the All-Purpose Room: "Professor Rossi! Annie! Come on up here!"—dab-dab-clap—"Don't be shy!"—dab-dab-clap—"Come on up!"

Annie's legs wobble, and she clings to her father on the high stage. There is a great deal of cheering (her ears are stuffed!), and there are cameras everywhere, with flashes popping everywhere. The kids from room 222 gather around, and they all talk at once—about whose page is here, whose page is there, whose is best, and so on.

And later, as Annie and her father walk down the steps of the Louis Armstrong School, there is another surprise. Snow! Snow! Snow! Falling from the sky in big white flakes. Annie looks down at her patent leather shoes. Uh-oh,

no boots . . . and whose fault is *that*? "Daddy"—clicking her tongue—"you were supposed to say, 'Don't forget your boots tonight, Annie.'"

"Ah, yes. Mommy *always* remembered boots." Professor Rossi rearranges Annie's scarf so that the snow doesn't slide down her collar. "And one of these days (let's hope), I'll remember, too."

Annie takes his hand and they start walking home, just the two of them, slipping sometimes and sliding sometimes, and snow pours over Broadway. They stop in front of Carmen's Diner. Happily, the lights are still on. Carmen's is a good place to warm up, they agree, and then they agree it's a very good night for pancakes. While they wait for pancakes in a booth with turquoise seats, Annie opens up to the very first page of **Remembering Mrs.**

Rossi. Slowly and together, Annie and her father turn the pages of their book. When they get to the end, they go back to page one and start again.

TWO

Annie's Blizzard

Like third graders everywhere, Annie Rossi has good days and bad days in school. A good day at Public School 88 is when they have something delicious (like hot dogs!) for lunch in the school cafeteria; or when a new girl (Jean-Marie) shows up in room 107 and your teacher (Miss Meadows) says (in front of the whole class!), "I think the best place for Jean-Marie is the seat next to *Annie Rossi*." A bad day, on the other hand, is *any* day you have to read about ugly old *reptiles* in science; or when you have to play *volleyball* in gym and you keep missing *everything* and no one picks *you* for a team.

Not surprisingly, Annie looks forward to an occasional day *off* from school. She especially loves the snowy days (*Come on, snow. . . . More, more snow!*), when they officially cancel school. This hardly ever happens . . . but one day that winter—finally—a fine big storm! All through the night, it sweeps across the city with noisy howling winds. By the time Annie opens her eyes the next morning, snow covers everything as far as she can see. Great big mounds of it! Best of all is the note on her bedside table. Annie and her father often leave each other notes around the house, many of which have something to do with chores, such as this one:

*Annie, please! Dirty clothes belong in the
hamper . . . and NOT on the bathroom floor!
Love, Daddy*

Or this one:

Dear Daddy,
You forgot to take me to the library.
Now my library books are LATE, and
Miss Madison will make you pay a fine.
Love, Annie

But on this snowy morning, the note Annie
finds has nothing to do with chores.

*Lucky you, Annie! No school today!
So go back to sleep.
Or better yet, join me for breakfast. . . .*

Annie springs off her bed and runs barefoot to the kitchen, where the wonderful smell of coffee fills the air. "I bet it's two feet deep, Daddy! No, three!" She slides into her seat near the window. "Can I have coffee," she asks, "in honor of my day off from school?"

"*May* I." Professor Rossi puts two bowls on the little white table that used to be set for three.

"*May* I, because last week you let me have coffee." (In fact, it had been mostly milk with a splash of coffee, barely a spoonful.)

"Are you sure it was me?" he teases. "Because I don't actually approve of children drinking coffee."

"It was you," Annie says. "Definitely."

"Well then"—shaking cereal into the bowls—"I must be an extremely nice fellow."

"*Extremely.*" Annie giggles.

Professor Rossi pours milk in Annie's glass, then coffee (just a splash). Then he picks up the morning paper and disappears behind it as usual. He always starts with sports. Then around-the-world news, and after that, city news. He does the same thing, in the same order, every single morning, and yet *this* morning it occurs to Annie that what he does is boring. She even feels a little sad on his behalf, *because* he is so boring. She also feels a little sad on her own behalf, because why can't he just be *fun* for a change? Surely other fathers are fun. Especially on such a special day, a day when they cancel school.

Annie gently knocks two knuckles on the table—*Knock, knock, Mr. Boring!*—then under the table: *Hello, hello! It's time to plan our snowy day!* The newspaper rustles, but nobody answers her sweet little knocks. Annie makes a face at the back of the newspaper (the kind of face certain grownups find *atrocious*). She makes another face, too, even more atrocious than the one before, and tries to remember if her mother was boring like this at breakfast. No. Definitely not. Mothers talk to their children at breakfast. "Drink your milk, Annie. We don't want to be late for school. . . ." Yes, mothers pay attention to a little girl and tell her all kinds of interesting news . . . "Guess what, Annie? An *author* is coming to room 222 today. . . ."

Annie's stomach rumbles hungrily. Maybe she should just go into the living room *alone* . . . and eat her breakfast . . . *alone.* Who would even notice her empty seat at the table? No one! She pictures her skinny little self, eating her cereal all by herself in the living room in front of the TV. . . . "In Jean-Marie's house, there's a TV in the kitchen," Annie says to the back of the

34

newspaper. "*She's* allowed to watch before school."

"Mm-hmm."

"Maybe we should have a TV in the kitchen, too." Annie knows exactly how her father feels about this particular subject, but she likes waiting for him to say, "I certainly don't think we need a TV in *our* kitchen, Annie."

"I certainly don't think we need a TV in *our* kitchen, Annie."

"You *always* say that." Annie leans on her elbow and looks out the window at the snow-covered park. She needs to go to the park! Now! With her sled and red mittens and . . . "Okay, Daddy"—suddenly bossy—"I'm going to tell you exactly what we do today. It's a really good plan, so when will you be finished eating breakfast? Because we have to go to the park. Right away. We have to get there first. . . ."

"Can't, Annie." Professor Rossi puts down the paper. "I'm teaching this morning."

"Daddy"—smiling patiently—"it's a *no-school* day."

"Ah! *You* may have no school today . . . but *some* people have to work today." Professor Rossi shrugs good-naturedly. "Snowstorm or not, the university's open."

"But we're going to the park," Annie protests. "There's all that new *snow* in the park and we have to get there *first*."

"We'll go later," he promises. "After my classes."

Later? No, they have to go now. Because *later* there are other things to do. Annie picks up her spoon and pokes at her breakfast cereal. (He forgot to buy *her* kind again, so now she has to eat *his* kind again, and that means picking out the raisins.) "You could call in sick," she suggests. "Like the time you had that cough."

"But I don't have a cough."

"You *could* pretend." Annie puts four raisins in a napkin and rolls up the napkin.

"By the way, Annie, Mrs. Peterman is going to keep you company while I'm in school."

"I don't like Mrs. Peterman. I don't like any babysitters, and you know it." This is not altogether true, of course. Mrs. Peterman lives upstairs in apartment 12A and is a really *nice* babysitter, a babysitter who plans really good snacks for after school and lets Annie watch TV, even *before* she starts her homework. (Mrs. Peterman's favorite soap opera, *The Days and the Nights,* is currently Annie's favorite thing to watch, too.)

"Baloney," her father is saying. "Mrs. Peterman has always been like a grandma to you."

"She's not my grandma," Annie grumbles. "I don't even have a grandma."

"Fine, but you still need to spend the day with her. And *I* need to spend the day with my kids over at Sherman Hall."

"They're *not* your kids." Annie stomps off to her room. She closes the door hard (in fact, it is a slam) and throws herself on the bed and puts her face in the crumpled-up pillow to be sad for a while. *Nobody in this house cares about me,* Annie thinks sadly. *I'll have to find another house, where people are NICE, not MEAN. I'll run away from home and SOMEONE will be sorry.* She rolls off the pillow and wraps her arms around her knees, wondering where in the world she might run away to—and that's when she notices her pajama top is *red* plaid and the bottoms are *green*!

Well, now she feels stupid on top of everything else for wearing mismatched pajamas. Annie's lip begins to quiver. She covers her eyes with both hands, but still the tears jump out—so many tears, and so many reasons for tears! Because her pajamas don't match and they always used to. Because she had slammed a door. And because she wants to have fun with her *mother* today, and here she is stuck with a father who doesn't know you do certain things in a snowstorm. He doesn't know the rules.

"Honestly, Annie. I've never known you to be so *huffy*." A little while later, Professor Rossi is sitting on the edge of Annie's bed, trying to be silly by using words like *huffy*.

"I'm *not* huffy," Annie mutters, mopping her tears.

"Fine. But the door slamming has to go.

Makes me jumpy." In his silly voice, "Plus, we'll get a noisy-neighbor reputation."

"I *didn't* slam the door. The *wind* blew it."

"You don't say?" Eyebrows up.

"I'm very mad at you, Daddy."

"Oh, I *hate* when you're mad at me, Annie! It's so unpleasant!"

"Then don't go to work today. Stay home with your very own child."

"But what about my students?" Professor Rossi walks across the room to look out the window. "Think of them, Annie, trudging across campus in all that snow. Just to hear my *scintillating* lecture."

"You always use big words, and I *hate* when you use big words!" All at once Annie pulls herself to a standing position in the middle of her bed. "See these pajamas?" Turning slowly on the bed. "They don't *match*."

"You're absolutely right." Nodding. "They *don't* match."

"You're supposed to put the red top with *red* bottoms, not green."

"Yes, I need to try harder with that laundry," he agrees, "and perhaps you can show me again about the folding. You do *such* a good job folding laundry," he adds. "Anything else, Annie? And please, no more complaints!"

Annie slides off the bed. It just so happens she has *lots* of complaints! "Well, it's *boring* at breakfast when all you do is read the newspaper, that is complaint number one," Annie says calmly. "You always forget to buy *my* cereal, complaint number two."

"Yes, but I can explain about the cereal . . ."

Annie doesn't want his explanations. No sir, she wants to wave her arms in the air, this way and that, and tell her father all the hundreds of things he does wrong every day—all the *millions* of things he simply doesn't know! "We're supposed to be the *first* ones making tracks in the park . . . and then we come home and make cookies . . . and eat them hot . . . and that's what you do in a snowstorm. *Mommy* knows!" Annie blinks with surprise at her very own rush of words. *Mommy knows, Mommy knows. . . .*

Professor Rossi puts his arm around Annie. They look at the park and the snow-covered trees and don't say much for a while. Then Annie makes lines for tic-tac-toe on the window in the frost. "I don't even *like* tic-tac-toe—it's stupid," she mumbles when she doesn't win her game. She intends to pout and frown for a while, but just then the memory of *another* day pops into her head, and the memory makes her smile. "Remember the time I went to school with Mommy in a snowstorm? Remember, Daddy? I got to go to sixth grade!"

"You were five, as I recall. Very spunky," adds Professor Rossi, "going off with your mom to the big school."

"Did everyone think I was cute, all the big kids?"

"Apparently, you were quite a hit with the sixth grade. We had a hard time getting you back to kindergarten after that!" Professor Rossi laughs. "Yes," he says, "you were simply crazy about Mommy's class."

"And Mommy was simply crazy about *me*."

"You bet," her father says softly, "and me."

Annie pats his wrist. "Don't be sad," she says. "I'll go to school with you sometime, too."

"I suppose . . ." Professor Rossi rubs his chin. "No, never mind . . ."

"Never mind *what*?"

"Oh, it's just a silly idea. You know me and my silly ideas."

"Maybe it's a good idea," Annie says. "Tell it, Daddy!"

"Okay, then, here's my idea. Since your school is closed today, you *could*—if you want—come to school with me."

"You mean *now*?" Annie gasps.

"Mm-hmm."

"And no Mrs. Peterman? Just you and me?"

"Just you and me," he says. "Plus a bunch of college kids. And if you care to do a little spy work," he adds, lowering his voice, "you will surely catch at least one sleeper in my nine o'clock class. There's always one who dozes."

"Well, Daddy, I hope it's not boring in your nine o'clock class."

"*Boring?*" Professor Rossi pretends to be

44

shocked. "As a matter of fact—and you'll see firsthand—I happen to be a scintillating, *interesting* teacher. And remember, Annie, you have to laugh at my jokes. You can't fall asleep, either."

"Too many rules!"

"Oh, one more thing. We'll have cookies in my office later on, and tea."

"I don't like tea," Annie reminds her father.

"You *could* pretend. Now hurry up and get ready." Professor Rossi kisses the tip of Annie's nose. Then he goes inside to call off Mrs. Peterman.

Annie quickly dresses: gray skirt, red sweater, warm socks. She brushes her short hair. She brushes her teeth and washes her cheeks and examines the scar on her chin. (It is lovely.) At the front door, she pulls on her boots and coat. It's time to go to college! Well, nearly. Annie races back to her room. She reaches under the mattress, wriggling her fingers until she feels the familiar cardboard cover of **Remembering Mrs. Rossi**. *Hello there, best book in the world.*

They aren't the first ones in new snow this morning, and they don't go to the park. Nonetheless, Annie and her father make beautiful tracks, and they both carry school bags. Professor Rossi's is crinkled and brown; Annie's is blue with a red handle, and **Remembering Mrs. Rossi** is tucked safely inside. They tramp along in deep snow. They trudge up the steep hill to Broadway, through the tall iron gates, and onto the campus of Columbia University. Sherman Hall is five stories tall, and they clomp up the stairs (too many stairs!) to the very top floor, to room 505. Professor Rossi turns on the light.

"It's so big!" Annie whispers. "Way bigger than room 107." She looks around at the walls with no pictures. (There are many pictures on all the walls in room 107.) There are no cubbies, either, and no class pet. (Everyone has a cubby in room 107, and they all share the goldfish, Walter and Sue.) In room 107 Annie always sits at the second desk in the third row. In room 505 there are rows and rows of dark wooden desks, and Annie is allowed to sit wherever she wants. From 8:45 a.m. until 8:55 a.m., she tries out seven different desks in seven different rows. In the end she settles on one in the very last row, right under the clock—a perfect spot for spy work.

The college kids burst in shaking snow off their coats, stamping wet boots. (Three kids aren't even wearing boots!) Some say, "Morning,

Professor Rossi," and others say, "Hi." (Some say nothing at all!) The college kids are tall, short, and medium in height. (Two of them look like grownups!) They drop into seats, in groups big and small, talking and laughing. (A few sit alone.)

On the dot of nine o'clock, Professor Rossi steps forward, and—just like that—a hush falls over room 505. (In room 107 it is never quiet—not even for a second—not until Miss Meadows says, "Quiet down, people.")

"I'm pleasantly surprised to see that so many of you made it to class on such a stormy morning." Professor Rossi smiles in a friendly way as he looks around the room. (Annie sincerely hopes the students like his friendly smile.) "I suppose," he goes on with a laugh, "you couldn't *bear* to miss my fascinating little

talk on Romeo and Juliet in a modern world."
(Annie hopes *someone* will laugh at her father's
joke. But nobody laughs.)

Professor Rossi clears his throat. "Ladies,
gentlemen." He clears his throat a second time,
and you can tell he is about to say something
important. "I wanted to let you know we have a
visitor in class today. A student from another
school," he adds, "and a real charmer, if I may say
so myself. Her name is *Annie. Annie Rossi*" (as if
it is the most important name in the world!).
"She is eight years old and—*be forewarned*—she
is watching everything you do."

Annie feels her face getting red. Everyone
turns to look at her. A few even wave to her!

For the next hour, Professor Rossi talks
about Romeo. He talks about Juliet. He does not
talk about Annie. (Frankly, she is hoping to hear

at least one little story about herself.) He walks back and forth, and up and down the aisles. Annie doesn't actually care all that much about Romeo, or even Juliet. She pumps her feet back and forth in big black boots, counting the students in Room 505. (There are forty-six.) She counts the girls in room 505. (There are twenty-one.) And the girls with curly hair. (There are eight.) She counts the boys who keep their coats on in school. (There are six.) And the girls in red sweaters. (There are two, plus Annie.)

Annie's cheeks are cold and hot from the storm outside and the steam heat inside. She leans on her left elbow awhile, then her right elbow. She leans on both elbows and looks inside her school bag, on the floor near her feet, and reaches down, slowly, for her book. She puts it on her lap and looks around the room. *See what I have, everyone?* **Remembering Mrs. Rossi** . . . *a whole book about my mother!* She smiles as she pictures herself reading out loud to the college kids, all of them squeezing as close as they can to Annie. They love her book very much, and they love Annie very much, and two— no, *five*—of the big girls want to be her friend! *Please, Annie, please! Be my best friend. . . .*

Annie opens her book for the hundredth— no, *thousandth*—time. She reads slowly. Silently. Quietly turning the pages. *Hello, Mommy. It's me, Mommy. . . .* Page after page, like so many secret little visits with her mother, and she imagines, just for a moment, a tiny version of herself dancing on the pages with her mother . . . and their fingers are touching, and no one dies. . . .

Now and then Annie pauses, determined to choose, once and for all, her *favorite* story. But she runs into the same old problem every time: how to pick the *best* story when every single one is the best in the world. Twenty-four stories and twenty-four best authors!

Once she wrote a letter to the authors in room 222, all twenty-four. The letter was her father's idea ("We need to write a proper thank-you, Annie, for our book about Mommy"), but *she* did all the work—including lots of good pictures by Annie.

Dear Alex, Benny, Carrie, Charlie, Drew, Frankie, Herman, Jake, Joe, Julie, Justine, Leo, Liliana, Lola, Louise, Matthew, Miriam, Olivia, Peter, Sabrina, Sal, Sofia, Tess, and Yelena:

Thank you for making a book about Remembering Mrs. Rossi. It's my favorite book, and you are my favorite authors. Guess how many times I've read my book? Answer: one million. Okay. This is true. A book about your mother makes you feel cozy as cocoa inside. Okay, this is funny. One time I was reading <u>RMR</u> in the bathtub, and it almost fell in! I never did that again. Guess which is my FAVORITE page? Answer: ALL of them! This is secret. Sometimes late at night, my father thinks I'm sleeping, but I'm not! I am reading <u>Remembering Mrs. Rossi.</u> I read and read. It's like giving my mother a kiss good-night. And she is giving me a big kiss too.

From,
Annie Rossi, age 8 ½
P.S. My father likes it, too.

Annie rests her head on her hands on the dark wooden desk. She drums her fingers softly on the desk and imagines running home to tell her mother all about her day off from school. *Mommy, there's a girl in Daddy's class with long red hair . . . and two girls were telling secrets . . . and a boy with a silly green hat was sleeping, I think.*

Professor Rossi talks on, and Annie drums on, longing to tell her mother about no hot cookies and mismatched pajamas and her big black boots making beautiful tracks all the way to Sherman Hall. Yes, she longs to tell her mother every single thing about the biggest blizzard ever, and together they can give it a name. They can call it *Annie's Blizzard.*

THREE

The Birthday

One spring morning, Annie Rossi escorts her father to the breakfast table. The inside of her is bubbling with excitement. On the outside, though, she is trying to sound wise and serious. "In honor of your birthday," she says in a wise-and-serious tone of voice, "*I'm* in charge of breakfast, and *you* have to do everything I say."

"Everything?"

"Yes"—Annie nods—"and you may now sit down."

Professor Rossi sits in his usual seat across from Annie at the table. Because it is such a *special* day (all birthdays are), Annie has already set the table and made breakfast— including toast and blueberry jam (her father's favorite). She has even put his news- paper on the table (open to his favorite page, sports).

"As you can see," Annie says, "someone has been hard at work this morning."

"Yes, and I certainly am impressed." (Her father is impressed!) "Looks good enough to eat," he adds, passing the jam to Annie.

"Also as you can see, someone is not wearing boring old school clothes today. Someone is wearing her *good* dress for your birthday."

"Yes, I noticed right away. And your good shoes, too."

"Did you notice anything else," Annie asks

modestly, "such as two chocolate milks on the table? Because someone made them before, when you were in the bathroom shaving."

"Well, *someone* must be a mind reader. Because if there's one thing I'm in the mood for, it's chocolate milk." Professor Rossi takes a long and surprisingly noisy drink. "Outstanding!"

"You may now tell me all about our Yankees." From time to time—even when it isn't her father's birthday—Annie pretends to be interested in baseball. She likes to pretend she is a big Yankee fan. (Her father, a *genuine* Yankee fan, seems to appreciate this.)

"Unfortunately"—big frown as he scans the headline—"our Yankees managed to lose again last night."

"Oh *dear.*" Annie drags her chocolate milk through a straw, inch by inch, to make it last.

"It all fell apart at the bottom of the ninth." Professor Rossi shakes his head and begins to explain exactly how it fell apart. "With bases loaded, the last thing you want, Annie, is a high pop toward center field—"

"Okay, Daddy, now we should talk about something *happy*." Annie cuts him off, but in the brightest possible way. "And I know just the thing that makes *everybody* happy—birthday presents!"

"You've got to watch out for sloppy hitting," her father informs Annie.

"Daddy, we already stopped talking about baseball," Annie reminds him sweetly. "Now, I've been thinking"—extra-sweet—"a *dog* makes a good birthday present, and I bet you want a dog!" (In fact, she has already practiced saying these very words—several times—in front of the bathroom mirror.)

Professor Rossi slowly lowers the paper until it is face-down on the table.

"I know a lot about dogs," Annie rushes in. "If you want, I could even help you pick one out!"

"Annie. *Must* we have this conversation again?" He sighs. "We've had it so many times already. Dozens of times over the years . . . no, *hundreds.*"

"A dog is fun," Annie says.

"Yes, but—"

"A dog is your friend," Annie says. "Some dogs are brave!"

"Yes, but some *people* aren't that comfortable with dogs, and, as you well know, I happen to be one of them."

"That's not fair!" Annie bangs her elbows on the table. "You *never* like my good ideas!"

"Don't pout, Annie." Professor Rossi spreads

extra jam across his toast and takes two big bites.

"*Everyone* has a dog."

"Everyone does not have a dog, and you know it."

"Well, the super's boy—that boy in Mommy's class—he got a puppy, and I got to hold the puppy in the lobby. Did you know *that*?"

"I seem to remember a nice long story about a puppy with silky ears." Professor Rossi smiles.

Annie does not smile back. He's *supposed* to want a dog for his birthday! He's *supposed* to be nice, not mean! "Your birthday's not fun anymore"—Annie jabs at her toast—"and *you're* not fun." She had cut all the toast into beautiful triangles for his birthday, and he didn't even notice.

Suddenly, Annie is tired of her father's birthday, tired of chocolate milk, and tired of being in charge. It seems to her she's just no good at it, and why couldn't her mother be in charge of birthdays like always? Everyone has a mother, and she wants one, too. She wants her very *own* mother, now! "*Mommy's* fun," she blurts out, "and Mommy had a dog when she was a little girl—did you know *that?*"

"A dog?" Professor Rossi seems quite surprised.

"Yes," Annie says in her know-everything tone of voice.

"A dog?" he repeats. "Are you sure? Because I thought I knew everything about Mommy, and I never heard about—"

"*I* know everything about Mommy. And *I* know she had a dog. A dog named Miss Phoebe, and I even have a secret picture to prove it!" (Annie doesn't actually mean to say that about the picture. Because now her father is going to say, "Where did you find this secret picture, Annie?")

"Where did you find this secret picture, Annie?"

Annie bites off a corner of her toast. She chews carefully, taking her time, so she doesn't have to say, "I found it in Mommy's top dresser drawer." If she says that, she might wind up saying, "Also I found big sunglasses there, and her lipstick is there, and I look pretty in Mommy's sunglasses . . . and once I tried on her lipstick and you didn't know, so *ha·di·ha* to you!"

"What a curious development," her father is saying. "I sure would like to see that picture sometime. . . ."

Annie folds her arms across her chest and pinches her lips into a straight line. It's *her* picture. She found it. Why should she show it to a mean old father who doesn't want a dog?

"Oh, here comes the long face! A long face on my birthday!"

He is trying to make her giggle but *too bad!* Annie pinches her lips a little more. She is not about to giggle, or smile, *or* show him her secret picture. Then again, it's such a *good* picture . . . and one teeny part of her (the part that simply *cannot* keep a secret) wonders if—maybe—one quick peek would be okay. Only, *she* has to be in charge . . . *See this little girl hugging her dog? This one, Daddy, with a flower in her hair. See, she has short hair like me! And freckles like me! But her eyes are green and mine are brown, and that's how you know she's Mommy! And now, look here. Because here in the corner, someone wrote: THELMA (AGE 10) WITH HER DOG, MISS PHOEBE . . .*

"Okay, *fine.*" Annie pushes back her chair. "*Fine,*" she repeats. "I'll show you the picture of Mommy."

She finds it in her sock drawer between two pairs of white summer socks. The window is open and the day is bright, and a breeze blows in the window. Down in Riverside Park, a boy and a lady run with a dog. *Is that your mother, little boy? Hey! What's your dog's name, little boy?* Annie smiles but it's a sad little smile because the boy has a dog to play with and she does not. The boy has a mother . . . and no one feels lonely down there.

Annie turns from the window and plants a little kiss on the picture of her mother. "I love *you,*" she whispers, "and I love Miss Phoebe . . . and *Daddy* is mean." Annie sits on the floor to pack up her things for school, including her spelling notebook, with her picture tucked safely inside—a picture she no longer intends to share with a mean old father who doesn't like dogs!

Later that morning in room 107, Miss Meadows puts ten long-division problems on the blackboard. "Quiet down, people! It's time to practice our long division, so take out your math notebooks, please!"

Annie reaches into her desk for her notebook. Long division, *phooey*.

"Carefully copy each problem, and do not rush, boys and girls. When we rush, we make careless errors."

Annie turns to a clean page in her math notebook and copies the first problem at the top of the page. (340 ÷ 17). She writes neatly and sits back to admire her neat numbers but wishes it were spelling time instead. Annie happens to be an *excellent* speller, and spelling, in her opinion, is an *important* third-grade subject. (Arithmetic, in her opinion, is not important at all.) Every week Miss Meadows puts fifteen new words on the board, along with the homework assignment:

Spelling Homework:
1. Write each word five times in your spelling notebook.
2. Write down an interesting sentence for each new word.

While Annie is not a big fan of homework in general, she doesn't actually mind *this* homework. As a matter of fact, she puts a big effort into her fifteen sentences each week. Sometimes, after an *especially* big effort, they come out sounding like a *story* . . . and Miss

Meadows says, "Well done, Annie! Now, how about reading your story to the class!"

"This is not a test, boys and girls." Miss Meadows walks up and down the aisles. "But we must do our best at all times."

Annie likes to do her best at all times. On the other hand, you can't always be in the mood for long division. With that thought in mind, she reaches inside her desk. (A good spy like Annie never gets caught!) Inch by inch, she pulls out her spelling notebook and puts it on her lap, where Miss Meadows can't see. (The good spy finds her secret picture.) *Hello again little girl who looks like me! We don't like long division, do we? Hello, Miss Phoebe!*

Annie quickly puts back the picture. (The good spy did *not* get caught). She still isn't in the mood for long division, though, and just for the fun of it, she reads over last night's spelling sentences, all of which please her very much. *Well done, Annie. Take a bow!* Why, *no one* in her class writes better sentences than she does! No one in the whole third grade—the whole *school,* and perhaps she should be an *author* one day when she's a grown-up lady!

Until this very moment, Annie has always assumed she will be a famous movie star one day. But an *author*! Why, authors get to make up sentences every day. They get to make up whole stories every day! Annie the author! How exciting! She will need a lot of red notebooks, of course, fountain pens, too—and a dog! Yes, indeed, an important author like Annie *absolutely* needs a dog.

"Number seven, Annie?"

Annie looks up. Seven. Seven what?

"Could you please tell us the answer to problem number seven?" Why is Miss Meadows looking at her like that? Annie closes the book on her lap, and maybe she stops breathing. You could hear a pin drop in room 107.

Miss Meadows is walking slowly up the aisle. "We're waiting." Closer! Closer! And now she is here! Right here at her desk!

Annie swallows, throat dry, and why is her face so hot? Burning hot!

"I'm disappointed in you, Annie," Miss Meadows says in a faraway voice.

Disappointed! Annie's stomach flops over. She looks down, down: Miss Meadows's feet in blue shoes.

"Now, may I please have that notebook?" Miss Meadows is saying. "The one on your lap."

With shaky hands and without looking up, Annie hands over her spelling notebook. *Don't cry! Don't cry! Don't cry!*

"Under the circumstances, Annie, recess is out of the question today. You can devote that time to your long division." Miss Meadows walks crisply to the front of the room. "You can collect this at three o'clock," says Miss Mean. She puts the notebook (and Annie's picture!) on her desk, underneath her Daily Lesson Planner.

"*I'm disappointed in you, Annie.*" Miss Meadows's words don't go away as the morning drags on. Miss Meadows stole her spelling notebook! She stole her mother's picture . . . and what if she never gives it back? Then what? Annie will just have to *tell* on her, *that's* what. She'll tell the *police,* and Miss Meadows will go to jail! Too bad for you, Miss Mean. . . .

Instead of going outside for recess, Annie goes to the school office. And there she sits, all by herself on a hard bench, unappreciated and slaving away at stupid long division while everyone else in room 107 is having fun. Anyway, who cares about stupid old school! Maybe she'll *quit* school! Miss Meadows will cry and cry. *Annie, we miss you so much! Look, we have your trophy! See what it says? MOST APPRECIATED THIRD GRADER, MISS ANNIE ROSSI!*

Afterward, after the *worst* recess in the history of her life, Annie slides into her seat in the third row. Jean-Marie holds up a tiny little sign in her own boxy print that says: RECESS IS NO FUN WITHOUT YOU. Annie loves the sign. But she refuses to look at Miss Meadows. *Excuse me, Miss Mean, have you heard my good news? I am quitting school!* Most days Annie raises her hand quite a lot in school, but for the whole rest of *this* day, she decides *not* to raise her hand — and something else she decides: no smiling. No sir, she'll never smile again in room 107 — no matter what. The afternoon drags on . . . 2:05 . . . 2:10 . . . 2:14 . . . On the dot of three, Annie runs out of the classroom. She does not say, *See you tomorrow, Miss Meadows,* on her way out the door. Nor does she "collect" her spelling notebook.

Nowadays Mrs. Peterman picks up Annie after school. They take a slow walk home, stopping here and there to look in shop windows on Broadway. Rainy days they huddle close under Mrs. Peterman's red umbrella. As a rule, they discuss two things on their walk: first, Annie's day at school and, second, what to have for a snack. Mrs. Peterman waits in the same place in the schoolyard for Annie every day . . . and every day, in a private little place in her heart, Annie hopes and prays someone else might be there. If only—even once—her mother would be there, waving to Annie and blowing kisses across the schoolyard. *If only.*

Today, because she has had a very bad day, Annie does something highly unusual in the schoolyard. She throws her arms around Mrs. Peterman at the waist. Mrs. Peterman hugs

Annie tight for a while. "I'm glad to see you, too," she says.

"We will *not* talk about school today," says Annie.

"Not one juicy story?" Mrs. Peterman looks surprised.

"Nope." Annie shakes her head.

So they walk uptown and don't say a word about school. They discuss instead the warm spring day. They count baby carriages on Broadway. Annie tries very hard not to think about the third grade, but now and then she hears herself sigh a sad little sigh that means: *Miss Meadows doesn't like me anymore. . . .* As they approach the corner of 109th Street, though, she is momentarily distracted by the sight of cup-cakes in the window of Carmen's Diner.

"Mmmnn." Annie licks her lips. "Yummy cupcakes."

"I'm a big fan, too," admits Mrs. Peterman. "Cupcake. Just say the word and I'm first in line — morning, noon, night. Halloween, Christmas, birthdays . . ."

Birthdays? All at once something terrible occurs to Annie. TODAY IS HER FATHER'S BIRTHDAY . . . AND NOBODY MADE HIM A CAKE!

"Mrs. Peterman." Annie looks up. "Today is my father's birthday."

Mrs. Peterman nods, as if she already knows.

A birthday with no cake, why that's the saddest thing in the world! And it's all her fault, because she didn't bake him a cake! Then again, she doesn't know *how* to bake a cake . . .

"Did you hear what I said, Annie? Because I've just come up with a fine idea."

No, she did not hear. Why, why, *why* didn't she bake her father a cake?

Now Mrs. Peterman is repeating her fine idea: instead of going home today as usual, why not visit Annie's father in his office?

"But he's *working*, Mrs. Peterman. We can't interrupt him at work."

"Sure we can." Mrs. Peterman flicks her hand in the air. "Birthdays are just as important as work, don't you think so, Annie? Why, even important teachers at important universities need to find a reason to *celebrate* from time to time."

"Mrs. Peterman." Suddenly, Annie brightens. "We *could* bring cupcakes, if you want. To my father's office, if you want . . . for a big surprise!"

"Like I always say"—Mrs. Peterman puts her arm around Annie as she leads her inside, to the takeout counter at Carmen's—"great minds think alike."

By the time they get to the university gates (with three chocolate cupcakes in a box with yellow ribbon), Annie is *nearly* in a good mood. By the time they get to Sherman Hall, she *is* in a good mood. And by the time they find her father's book-lined office (room 202), she is absolutely *giddy*. They walk right in and yell, "Surprise!"

Professor Rossi is *so* surprised he nearly jumps out of his chair! "Well, look who's here! How about this! I've got company! The best company in the world!" He keeps scratching his head in confusion. "To think you two *innocents* cooked up such a sneaky little plan!"—he laughs—"And here I was, thinking just this minute, *If only I had something to eat, preferably chocolate!*"

Afterward—after they eat the cupcakes and sing the happy birthday song, and after Professor Rossi blows out pretend birthday candles—Mrs. Peterman taps her wristwatch with two fingers in a gesture that means it's time to go home. "Come along, Annie." Her tone is pleasant but has an edge of *authority*. "We have to let your father get back to work now."

"I better stay here, Mrs. Peterman." Annie's tone is pleasant, too. She smiles at Mrs. Peterman.

"Now, Annie . . ."

"My father shouldn't be *lonely* on his birthday." As the words slide sweetly off her tongue, Annie hopes everyone in the room will recognize what a nice girl she is—a girl who chooses to keep her father company on his birthday, instead of watching TV! (Annie would prefer keeping him company at the playground, of course, or perhaps in a movie theater, but her father has already explained—several times—about his teaching *responsibilities* here at Columbia

University, including his 4:30 responsibility, which has something to do with creative writing.)

A few minutes later, having successfully persuaded the grownups to let her stay, Annie makes herself at home at her father's important-looking desk. She sits in his big black chair, feeling terribly important herself as she watches him pack up for his 4:30 class. "By the way," she says casually, "I'm quitting school, Daddy. You'll never talk me out of it, so don't even try."

"Quitting school is serious business," he responds in a not-too-serious tone of voice. "I would be remiss if I didn't at least *try* talking you out of it."

Annie leans forward on her knees and types her name on his old-fashioned typewriter. But typing is hard and it comes out *anine*. It seems to her (except for the cupcakes) this whole day is hard.

Grownups! They spoil everything! A father who doesn't want a dog for his birthday. A teacher who says, "I'm disappointed in you, Annie," and steals your picture of your mother . . .

Annie prints Annie was here on her father's desk calendar on today's page. She makes a picture of a dog on tomorrow's page, then another dog, right next to the first one, and now no one is lonely.

A few minutes later, they are clattering down the stairs. In light of the perfect spring day, Professor Rossi has made arrangements for his 4:30 class to meet *outside* today, under a tree.

"Do you want to know *why* I'm quitting school?" Annie asks as they walk across the grass.

"I'm always curious to know why you do the things you do, Annie."

"Because Miss Meadows doesn't like me anymore, that's why!"

"Really?"—big frown—"I was under the impression she likes you immensely."

"She used to," Annie says. "But not anymore. I never had a teacher who didn't like me before," she adds gravely. "Miss Kim used to like me. Every single day of second grade."

"Miss Kim was a big fan," Professor Rossi agrees.

"And do you remember Mrs. Levine? She was my first-grade teacher, and she liked me a lot. Even the time I said Pamela Miller was fat, she didn't stay mad." Annie sighs. "Mrs. Levine understood a little first grader couldn't be perfect every second of the day."

"Yes, Mrs. Levine understood a great many things about first graders."

"Miss Meadows doesn't understand anything at all about third graders." Annie is getting sadder by the minute.

"Professor Rossi! Over here!" The group her father calls his Senior Writing Seminar kids are waiting under a big leafy tree. These kids (according to her father) like writing stories, and every Tuesday someone gets to read his or her story to the rest of the class.

"Hello, writers!" Professor Rossi picks up his pace and calls, "Come on, Annie!"

"But I'm in the middle of *my* story," Annie mumbles as her father settles under the tree with his students. Apparently, their stories are more interesting than hers. Fine! She'll sit under another tree, then—a *nearby* tree, where she can spy on her father and his dumb old class. There are five boy writers and four girl writers lounging over there. Two of the boys and three of the girls have kicked off their shoes! Annie pulls off her shoes and puts them on the grass next to her school bag. She wraps her arms around her knees, crushing her good dress. Professor Rossi waves and Annie waves back. She makes sure it is a sad little wave so he remembers Miss Meadows doesn't like her anymore. Miss Meadows, who makes you go to the school office and sit there all by yourself during recess . . .

"Annie? Is that Annie Rossi?"

Annie squints into the late afternoon sun. *Miss Meadows?* Impossible. Not now. Not here at the university. Why, you never see your teacher in the *world!* Only in school.

"What a wonderful surprise!" And here she

is, Annie's very own teacher, sitting on the grass beside Annie, acting as if she hadn't been mean that very morning. "I *thought* I recognized your father with his class over there." *Smiling* of all things, and *pretending* to be friendly! "It must be so much fun to teach outside on a day like this . . ."

Maybe, if she weren't so mad at Miss Meadows, Annie would be friendly back. Maybe she would even *like* having her teacher all to herself. But, of course, she *is* mad, and she intends to *stay* mad for the rest of her life.

"By the way, Annie, I looked over your spelling homework this afternoon and, *bravo,* your sentences are wonderful," says Miss Meadows. "I was hoping you might read them to the class tomorrow. We all appreciate the way you turn your spelling homework into these *catchy* little stories."

"*Catchy little stories!*" Annie is beginning to feel a little less mad at Miss Meadows.

"Oh, and this fell out of your notebook." Miss Meadows digs in her school bag. "It seemed rather special, so I put it in my bag for safekeeping," she explains. "Here, Annie."

"My picture!" Annie gasps with relief. *Don't cry now! Not in front of your teacher!*

"Cute girl." Miss Meadows looks carefully at the picture, then Annie, then again at the picture. "She looks just like you."

"It's my mother," Annie whispers.

"I thought it might be," Miss Meadows whispers back.

Annie puts the picture in her blue school bag. It's best not to think about her mother right now. She needs to concentrate on something else—on making Miss Meadows like her again. *But how,* Annie wonders, *how, how, how?*

Miss Meadows likes children who are *kind* and children who show *respect*. Why, she is always telling the kids in room 107, "We must be *respectful* and *kind*, boys and girls!" But Annie *is* respectful! And *extremely* kind! Didn't she make breakfast today in honor of her father's birthday? And bring cupcakes to his office?

"Today is my father's birthday," Annie hears herself tell Miss Meadows. "We had cupcakes in his office. My idea," she adds with just the right touch of modesty, "so he wouldn't be lonely."

"I *adore* cupcakes," confides Miss Meadows. "And birthdays . . . and birthday presents!"

"Me, too," Annie confides right back. "Only this year I didn't give him a present."

"Oh!"

"We were supposed to get a dog. . . ." Annie is grim. "*That* was the plan."

"But?"

"*Some* people aren't that comfortable with dogs." Rolling her eyes to the sky.

"I assume *you* are a person who is very comfortable with dogs," guesses Miss Meadows.

"Yes."

Miss Meadows nods in a way that means *she* likes dogs, too, and then she says, "My father likes pictures." (Miss Meadows has a father!) "When I was a little girl, I often made him a picture for his birthday."

"*My* father likes books," Annie says. "I wish I could make him a book."

"Maybe you can."

"Only grownups write books, Miss Meadows." But even as she says it, Annie is thinking about another book, **Remembering Mrs. Rossi**. Grownups didn't write that! The kids in room 222 did!

"Maybe you could write a *short* book," suggests Miss Meadows. "Maybe"—thinking—"oh, here's an idea! How about a birthday card, Annie, with a story inside? A story by *Annie* inside!"

A story by Annie inside! Annie giggles at the thought of it. *Annie the author!*

"Ah, so you like my idea?" Miss Meadows looks pleased.

Annie nods. "But . . . what *kind* of story?"

"Hmmm." Miss Meadows wrinkles her nose and thinks. "Well"—more thinking—"it's always good to write about something you know," she points out. "Better yet, about *someone* . . . or maybe a whole *family* you know."

Annie opens her school bag. She takes out

her mother's picture again. "Maybe a story about my family," she says slowly, "and we get a dog . . . and . . ."

Miss Meadows blinks in the sunlight and moves a tiny bit closer to Annie. "What a wonderful idea!" She starts digging around in her big bag again. "Here, Annie, you can borrow this if you like, my favorite pen." She puts a very green and very fancy pen in Annie's hand. "A story this important deserves a special pen."

Annie's teacher is giving her a special pen!

"Just bring it back to school tomorrow." Miss Meadows stands up and brushes off her skirt. "Now *I* have to go to school," she says.

"You do?"

Miss Meadows points to Sherman Hall. "Right up there in room 303, that's where I'm taking one of those 'how to be a better teacher' classes. I'm always here at the university on Tuesdays," she says with a friendly shrug. "Always trying to be a better third-grade teacher."

Annie wants to say, *But you're the best third-grade teacher already!* She doesn't, though. After all, she is still a teeny bit mad at Miss Meadows.

The Rossis Get a Good Dog
by Annie Rossi

Once upon a time in New York City, there was a pretty lady. Her name was Mrs. Rossi and she was a teacher. But only sometimes. Most of the time she was someone's mommy, and her little girl was called by the name Annie. Annie was kind. She was a good speller. She wanted a dog. But Father said, "So sorry, no dogs." Annie was sad. Boo-hoo. Then she said to Father, "My mom had a dog when she was a girl." "She did not!" "Yes, she did! And here is a picture to prove it." "Okay, you win, Annie. Let's get a dog." So the Rossis got a dog and they all lived happily ever after for a million years. The good dog had a good name, too. Her name was Miss Phoebe.

Happy Birthday, Daddy!!

An hour past Annie's official bedtime, she is still sitting up in her bed, still a bit jumpy for sleep. Besides, it's important to go over everything one more time.

"Okay, Daddy. What was the best part of your birthday?" she asks. (She has already asked the same question. Several times.) "Your favorite part."

"There were quite a few favorite parts, Annie. There's your story, of course—which I have every intention of reading to my Senior Writing Seminar kids next Tuesday. Nobody ever wrote a story just for *me* before," he adds in a serious tone of voice.

"Let's talk about how *funny* my story is."

"Oh yes. It's quite amusing, Annie. Love that title! But beyond that, your story has *heart* and, as you well know, my very favorite stories are the ones with *heart*."

"And do you like how I put Mommy's picture on the cover?" (They have already talked about the cover. Several times.)

"Yes. It's the most wonderful picture of Mommy." Professor Rossi does not seem to tire of saying this. "To think, she once had a dog named Miss Phoebe! And to think, *you* were the one who figured it out! *Excellent* spy work, Annie."

"Are you sorry we didn't have a real birthday cake, the usual kind?" Annie worries. "Did it make you sad?"

"*Sad?* Baloney!" He laughs. "Why, that was the best cupcake I ever ate, ever! Scrumptious!"

"I don't know *how* to bake a real birthday cake," Annie says. And then, "Nothing's the same without Mommy."

"I miss her, too."

"Daddy. I forgot . . . I forgot to tell her." Annie feels a lump rising in her throat. "At the hospital that night . . . I forgot to say, *I love you.* . . . Now Mommy doesn't know!" Annie swallows and swallows, but the tears squirt out.

Professor Rossi picks up Annie's hand. He counts the fingers on her hand and slowly folds down each finger. "Oh, you said it, all right." He nods with conviction. "Not only that night, Annie, but as I recall—and I certainly *do* recall— you and Mommy were always saying, 'I love you, I love you, I love you!'"

"Really?" Annie whispers. "Do you promise?"

"Promise."

"Are you sure?"

"I'm sure."

"Daddy"—more worries—"what if I stop remembering Mommy?"

"We'll always remember Mommy," he says. "We always will, and *there* is another promise. Now sleep, Annie. Tomorrow's school. Unless, of course, you're still planning to quit school."

Annie yawns. "Maybe I'll go. Miss Meadows needs me," she explains. "She needs me to read to the class."

"Okay, then, I will see you in the morning."
Professor Rossi bends down and kisses Annie
on the top of her head, and then on both cheeks.

"Daddy?" Two more yawns.

"Yes, Annie?"

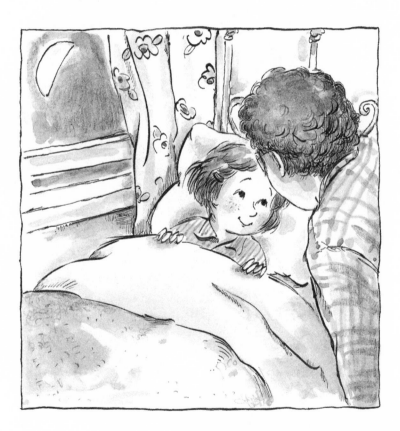

"You have to have *one* best thing about your birthday," she says. "One *favorite* thing."

"YOU." Professor Rossi turns off the light. "YOU are the best thing, definitely."

Annie sinks into her fluffy pillow. "Happy birthday," she says. "Good night!"

The window is open a crack, and the moon is right where it should be. There! In front of Annie's window! A big yellow half-moon, and she goes to sleep in the light of the half-moon.

FOUR

Summer People

Annie Rossi is trying to do a perfect handstand on the beach. *Feet up! Stay up! Feet up!* It is her fourth try this morning, her tenth try this week—her *hundredth* try this summer! "Maybe you're just not a handstand kind of girl," her father had said (several times), and perhaps he meant to be helpful. But his words had deeply offended Annie. Why *can't* she be a handstand kind of girl? Her friend Helen is quite accomplished in this regard. Helen lives next door every summer on Pineapple Street, and this summer she is *ten*. Whenever *she* does a handstand, her feet stay right where they should, high in the air, and she never flops over like Annie, who is still only 8¾. (Helen is also quite good at floating on waves. *And* backbends.) Annie knows she should be pleased to have a friend who is so accomplished, but deep down it annoys her.

Feet up! Stay up! Feet up . . . Yes, she's doing it! Then thunk. *She flops into the sand.* At this moment, however, *nothing* can spoil Annie's good mood—not even a *thousand* bad handstands in a row! After all, the sun is out. The sea is calm. Her bathing suit is pretty. And best of all, she has just met the brand-new baby on Pineapple Street. (The brand-new baby happens to be Helen's brother—which, Annie supposes, is just *another* accomplishment for Helen.) His name is James, and now that Annie has seen him with her very own eyes, all she can *think* about is James! All she wants to *talk* about is James!

"Did you see his little feet, Daddy, did you?" Annie drops to the sand beside her father.

"Mm-hmm." Professor Rossi is scribbling away in his brown notebook. (He's been doing that a lot on the beach this summer.)

"And how about those toes!" Annie exclaims, sprinkling sand on her father's long toes. "I've never seen such tiny toes before."

Professor Rossi looks up. "I seem to remember inspecting *your* toes, Annie, the day you were born."

"You did not!" Annie giggles.

"Ten fine toes." Professor Rossi chooses his

words, pretending to be ever so serious. "I found them *very* interesting," he says, waving his pencil in the air.

"What about Mommy? Did she inspect, too?"

"Mommy?" Professor Rossi's eyes are wide. "Why, Mommy was the inspector *general,*" he declares. "She was the boss of counting, Annie, and we counted *everything* that day—toes, fingers, ears . . ."

"And Mommy knew I was perfect. And she carried me all the way home . . . in my yellow baby blanket."

"Oh yes, Mommy knew a perfect baby when she saw one." Professor Rossi smiles briefly. Then he goes back to his notebook, back to being boring.

A nice new baby to play with, right next door! What could be better than that! *Well, a brother of my own* — the thought suddenly occurs to Annie — *that would definitely be better.* And the more she thinks about it, the more she wishes James could be *her* baby brother, not Helen's. It makes her mad somehow. Some people have all the luck — people like Helen.

Annie has been told many times, of course, and in many different ways, not to be jealous of someone else's good fortune. But it seems to her certain people (such as Helen Cooper) have *tons* of good fortune, while certain other people (such as Annie Rossi) do not. Helen Cooper is allowed to walk to town without a grownup! (Annie Rossi is not.) Helen Cooper is allowed to swim out to the second buoy! (Annie Rossi is not.) Helen Cooper has a subscription to *Movie Star* magazine! (Annie Rossi does not.) And now *this,* a baby brother. It just isn't fair. Annie lets out a very long sigh so that anyone nearby (such as her father) knows it isn't fair. But he is scribbling away and crossing out and scribbling and crossing out. Her sigh goes unnoticed.

"Well, good*bye,*" announces Annie, brushing sand off her legs.

"Goodbye?"

"Yes." She stands abruptly. "I have *work* to do."

"No kidding! You're actually going to make your bed today?"

"*No,* Daddy. I'm talking about *important* work, because the Coopers need my help with the baby."

"Ah." Her father looks up from *his* important work and nods. "They certainly did look a bit *frazzled* over there. Newborns have a tendency to wreak havoc, as I recall, in an otherwise normal household."

"Havoc, havoc, havoc!" Annie laughs as she races up the beach. She can't wait to get another look at that baby.

The Coopers have a porch and a door that creaks, just like the Rossis. Unlike the Rossis, they have a dog—Al. As a rule, Al spends his days running up and down the beach, in and out of the ocean. He barks often and happily. (He especially seems to enjoy barking at Professor Rossi.) At this moment though, standing next to Annie on the porch, Al is absolutely quiet. His nose is pressed against the screen door, and no part of him moves, not even his tail. Annie kneels down and puts her arms around Al, and together they look in the house. It is very dark inside.

"Hello?" Annie calls. "Anybody home?"

"Hi." Helen appears on the other side of the door.

Al scrambles to his feet. He begins to scratch at the door and whimper.

"I've just been holding James," Helen whispers. "He likes when I hold him."

"Can I hold James?" Annie whispers back, through the screen.

"Only family members get to hold him today. He's a newborn," Helen explains in a voice that makes her sound unmistakably wise.

"How about tomorrow?" Annie offers. "I could come over in the morning to hold him if you want. I could be here at seven."

Scratch, scratch, whimper (this, from Al).

"Cut it out, Al." Helen flicks two fingers on the screen. "There's a *baby* in here."

"I guess he wants to play with James." Annie smiles so Helen remembers they are *good* summer friends—*best* summer friends! "Can we come in?"

"Not now. James is sleeping," Helen explains in her new wise way.

"I won't make noise," promises Annie.

"I know. But you might have germs."

Germs! Annie sincerely hopes she doesn't have germs of any kind. Of course, if anyone would know about this sort of thing, it would be Helen. Just yesterday, she was plain old Helen. But now, Annie realizes, she seems to know all kinds of important things. And if she says Annie has germs, well, she probably *does*!

"I better go," Helen says from the other side of the door. "In case James wakes up. He likes if I'm there when he opens his eyes."

"Do you want to come down to the beach?" Annie smiles. "My father could take us swimming."

"Maybe later." Helen turns to go. "I'm a big sister now," (as if Annie needs reminding), "and

you know what *that* means. I have responsibilities."

"I have *responsibilities*," Annie tells Al in a tone
of voice that sounds very wise. They are sitting
on the Rossi's front porch, the two of them, in
the hammock. Annie is looking at pictures,
trying to decide which ones to put in her summer scrapbook. When she comes to a picture of
Helen doing a cartwheel on the beach, Annie
chooses *not* to put it in her scrapbook. "We
don't like Helen," she whispers cheerfully to Al.

Suddenly, the sun disappears behind a cloud.
Professor Rossi is still on the beach and still
going *scribble, scribble, scribble* in that old brown
notebook. But now he looks up and waves to
Annie. Annie waves back. "Hello!" she calls
across the sand. "I bet you want to go
swimming!"

Her father waves again. A wave that means, *Not just yet, Annie. I'm doing something* important *. . . Anyway, that ocean is looking a little too choppy right now for swimming. . . .*

Grownups! The most boring people in the world certainly are grownups. *Scribble, scribble, scribble,* all summer long. And they won't even let you see their boring old notebooks—they won't even let you peek—grownups and their big-deal secrets! "Some things I write are not for sharing, Annie. At least, not yet." Well, *fine.* Because it just so happens, *she* has secrets, too. Good ones! Annie rolls and rocks the hammock and starts to count her secrets:

Secret #1: Once, I threw my vitamin pill in the garbage and nobody found out!

Secret #2: I have a secret bag of cookies! Under my bed, shhh!!

Secret #3: Sometimes I pretend Mommy is

coming! She's coming on the train to Pineapple Street, and I meet her at the station for a big surprise!!

Secret #4: Helen Cooper is a brat.

Secret #5: I wish I didn't have to go to room 245 for fourth grade. In seventeen days it's the first day of school, and I wish I didn't have Mrs. Bailey for fourth grade. I only want Miss Meadows. I love, love, love third grade.

Annie's thoughts turn over and over . . . to the last day of third grade . . . and her report card . . . and the back of her report card, where Miss Meadows wrote all those nice things about Annie, words she knows by heart.

It has been a real pleasure having Annie in my class this year. Annie is a diligent worker who gets along well with others. Her stories are a joy to read and share. Annie

should work on her arithmetic skills this
summer. Good luck in fourth grade!
— *Miss Meadows*

Just before the final bell, Miss Meadows put her address on the board. "Keep in touch, boys and girls. Write me a letter! Even a short one! I would love to hear from you this summer." Suddenly it was three o'clock and just like that, third grade was over. The kids in room 107 screamed and cheered. Annie screamed and cheered, too, but she was only pretending to be happy about the last day of third grade. Miss Meadows gave everyone a hug on the way out the door. When it was her turn, Annie tried to say, *Have a nice summer, Miss Meadows.* But when she opened her mouth, nothing came out. She simply couldn't say goodbye to Miss Meadows.

Annie had every intention of writing a really

catchy letter to Miss Meadows on the first day of summer vacation. Unfortunately, she didn't get around to it that day, or the next, or the one after that. By the end of the first week of summer vacation, she still had not written her letter. Annie and her father took the train—just the two of them this year instead of three—away from the hot city and opened the cottage on Pineapple Street. The sea was beautiful and cool, but Annie missed looking for seashells on the beach with her mother.

She did write two letters, though. One to Jean-Marie. (Jean-Marie did not write back.) And one to Mrs. Peterman. (Mrs. Peterman did write back.) Weeks passed. From time to time, Annie thought about writing that letter to Miss Meadows. *Dear Miss Meadows,* she would write. *I miss you so much and I love you so much because you are nice and my mother was nice and I wish . . .*

but the thought of writing all that made her too sad . . . and Annie was trying her best not to be sad. Anyway, there was always something else to do. There was swimming to do; or finding new books at the library; or talking to Sam, her favorite lifeguard; or playing with Al and Helen; or having an ice cream in town with her father. Then one day, just last week, and for no particular reason, Annie sat down on the beach and wrote a letter to Miss Meadows. She wrote carefully, in her best penmanship. Later she read it out loud as she walked to the post office with her father, and they both agreed it was a very catchy letter.

Dear Miss Meadows,

Hi! It's Annie Rossi! Remember me? I am having a good time on my summer vacation.

We live in a cottage! I swim in the ocean!
I am making an Annie Rossi Summer Scrapbook, and I take lots of pictures for my
scrapbook. There's a funny one. It's Al the
neighbor dog barking at my father. Woof,
woof!! I like the one of me on the porch
eating an ice pop. You never wear shoes
around here and your toes are happy. I am
learning to cook grilled-cheese sandwiches.
If you come over, I could make you one.

From,
Annie Rossi

P.S. Here is a picture of me in my red
bathing suit. I hope you like the picture.

Annie drapes one leg over the side of the
hammock. (She needs to slow down the rocking

in order to think and calculate.) A whole week—
plus two days—since she mailed her letter.
That's *nine* days, and Miss Meadows *still* hasn't
written back! "What in the world is taking so
long?" she mumbles to Al.

Al barks something to Annie.

"What'd you say, Al? You think there's a
letter from Miss Meadows? Waiting at the post
office *now*?"

Al barks again.

"That's what I thought you said!" Annie
tumbles off the hammock.

Al tumbles, too, and they charge down the
beach to Annie's father. "Can we go to the post
office?" she calls as she runs. "Miss Meadows
wrote me a letter, and I can't wait to read it!"

"Yes, yes. Good idea." He is crossing
something out with his fat red pen. "We'll go a
little later, Annie, right after lunch."

"Well, I might go *now*." Annie watches Al romp in the choppy sea, stirring up the sea.

"What was that, Annie?"

"I might walk to town." Annie knows perfectly well she isn't allowed to walk to town without a grownup, but it's fun saying, "I might walk to town," to certain people who don't pay attention when you talk.

"You know perfectly well you aren't allowed to walk to town without a grownup." Her father sounds just slightly irritated. "We'll go after lunch," he repeats.

"Helen is allowed to go to town without a grownup."

"Is that so?" Professor Rossi frowns. "Well, I don't happen to approve," he says. "Nonetheless, Helen's parents make the rules for Helen, and *I* make the rules for you."

"You have too many rules."

Just then Al runs out of the water. He runs straight for them, barking at her father as usual. Professor Rossi, as usual, pays him no mind.

Al continues to bark.

"Make him stop, Annie."

"He's just trying to be friendly," Annie points out.

"What he's *trying* to do is annoy me."

"If you were just a teeny bit friendly," Annie says, "he wouldn't have to bark so much."

Professor Rossi drums his fingers on his notebook. Then he picks up a stick and throws it, hard, toward the water, calling, "There you go, Al! See?" he says to Annie. "I'm friendly."

"You're only trying to get rid of him," Annie says, as Al comes galloping back with the stick in his mouth. "That's a little bit *rude*, Daddy."

"He's a *dog*, Annie! You can't be rude to a dog." (Sadly, Professor Rossi doesn't understand anything at all about dogs.) "Now, could you and Al *kindly* amuse yourselves? Just a little longer, Annie. I'm trying to write something here."

"Are you getting ready for the first day of school, is that what you're doing?"

"No, Annie."

"Are you writing a letter?"

"No, Annie."

"Are you making a list of your favorite foods? I *love* making lists like that . . . and I always put *ice cream* at the top of my list . . ."

"Annie, *please!*"

"It's not fair! You never tell me anything, and I always tell you everything I write . . . and I bet what you're writing is *boring!*" Annie turns on her heels, squeaking both feet in the hot sand. "Come on, Al. Let's have *fun* with that baby."

✻

For the second time this morning, Annie and Al peer through the Coopers' screen door. This time, though, Annie has brought along her father's camera, and she is holding it behind her back.

"Anybody home?" she calls into the dark house. "It's Annie and Al!"

"Hi." For the second time this morning, Helen appears on the other side of the door. "I just gave James a bath."

"All by yourself?" Annie can't believe the good luck some people have.

Al begins to scratch at the door and whimper.

"My mother helped," Helen says. "But just a little."

Annie tries her best not to think about the fact that certain people have a mother in the house and certain other people do not. But it's hard when certain people go around saying "my mother this" and "my mother that" every minute of the day.

"Anyway, *I* did most of the work," Helen is saying. "I'm an excellent baby bather."

"Anyway, *I* have a surprise," Annie says to the baby bather.

"Is it candy?" Helen whispers.

"You'll see." Annie hopes she looks terribly mysterious through the screen. "But first, we have to come in."

Helen opens the door a crack. "Is it cupcakes?" Helen slips outside before Al can slip inside. There's a dog biscuit in her hand, and she gives it to Al.

"No," Annie says. "This is even better than cupcakes. I'm going to take a picture of James!" And just to make sure her surprise is a big hit with Helen, she adds, "Then I'll take a picture of *you* with James, and I'll put it in my scrapbook."

Helen walks to the edge of the porch and sits down. Annie sits beside her, and Al squeezes in the middle, chomping noisily on his biscuit. Helen puts her arm around Al. She kisses the top of his head. (Al pretends not to care about the kiss, and Annie knows why: he is mad at Helen for not letting him play with the baby.)

"I could take the picture *now* if you want. I have time," Annie says.

Helen shrugs the kind of shrug that means, *Who cares?*

"Maybe you should go get James," Annie suggests, "now that he's nice and clean."

Helen shrugs again. *Who cares?*

Annie sighs loudly. Helen is *so* annoying . . . and what is *she* being so grumpy about? *She's* the lucky one, the one with the brand-new baby brother in the house! Well, maybe it's all that *havoc* her father was talking about. Yes, it could be Helen just needs to hear something funny, and then she'll quit pouting . . . and then she'll get James, and Annie can take a picture. "Okay, this is funny," Annie says hopefully. "See, I really thought James was going to be a *girl!*"

"Me, too," Helen says sadly. "I thought her name would be Jenny."

"Well, I never knew a *boy* baby could be that cute," Annie admits.

"Cute?" Helen shakes her head. "He's not so cute when he's crying."

"All babies cry." Annie hopes she sounds older than 8¾.

"Not as much as this one."

"I wish I had a baby . . . a baby sister." *And*

she wouldn't cry . . . and my mother and I would give
her a bath. . . .

Helen looks off in the distance, then up at
the sky. "My parents like him better," she says to
the sky.

Annie gasps. "Are you *sure?*"

Helen nods. She is sure. "Look, Annie!"
Helen points to the ocean. "It's really rough
now. I hope there's a big storm," she says. "I
love a big storm, don't you?"

"And thunder and lightning!" As a matter of
fact, Annie doesn't care for big storms at all, and
even the little ones scare her sometimes. But it is
important to side with Helen—now that her
parents don't like her so much anymore.

"Maybe I'll go away," Helen says wistfully.
"Nobody would even care."

"We could go to town!" The words fly out

of Annie's mouth, and the very sound of them sends shivers of excitement up and down her spine. "We could *walk* to town." She chooses her words carefully. "I'm expecting a letter from my teacher," she explains in a rather *wise* tone of voice. "We'll go to the post office for my letter."

Afterward Annie thinks about all the things she might have done differently. First of all, she would have worn shoes on her walk into town, and no one would call her *slowpoke*. (Helen wore shoes.) She would have chosen a different sort of day, too—a day without thunder and lightning. A day without soaking rain. Of course, Annie had no way of knowing all those fast gray clouds overhead would burst *just* as she and Helen turned onto Main Street. How could she possibly know a thing like that? And had she known the rain would make her so cold, she would surely have taken a sweatshirt. A nice cozy one—extra-long to her knees—to wear over her bathing suit. (Helen wore her sweatshirt—extra-long—over *her* bathing suit.)

"Help!" Helen is the first one to shriek, with the first bolt of lightning.

Annie shrieks, too, but of course she isn't *nearly* as frightened as Helen. Well, thank goodness for Al—good old Al, soaked to his bones. Annie smiles reassuringly at Al, so he knows everything will be okay. "Come on!" she calls. "Library!"

Annie and Helen and Al run to the other side of Main Street in the rain. They run up the library steps. The library has a tall green door. Annie has come and gone through this door many, many times in her life, but this is the first time she notices the sign: SHOES AND PROPER ATTIRE REQUIRED. NO BATHING SUITS!

"We can't go in." Annie swallows. "It's against the law."

They huddle close on the steps outside the library. Annie's teeth chatter and clack, and the rain pours down. Al is not used to huddling in the rain and doesn't seem to like it one bit. He scuttles to his feet and barks his goodbyes. Then he runs down the steps and runs to the end of Main Street. Without looking back, he turns the corner and disappears.

"Don't be scared." Annie's tone is brave. "I know what to do."

"I'm *not* scared."

Annie smiles a teeny little *secret* smile. Helen is lying, of course. Look who's ten and oh-so-frightened! "If you play a *game* when you're scared," Annie tells Helen, "it helps." (She says it loud, with her hands on her ears, in case there is more thunder.)

"I already told you, I'm *not* scared." Helen's sweatshirt covers her knees, and her knees aren't shaking with cold like Annie's. "What kind of game?"

"There's a good one called *secrets*." In fact, Annie has never actually heard of, or played, a game called *secrets,* but she likes the way it sounds.

"How do you play?"

"We have to tell each other a secret *confession*," Annie explains, as if she has played this game hundreds of times.

"But why?" Helen's sweatshirt has a hood, and her hair isn't dripping wet like Annie's.

"Because if we tell each other a secret *confession,* it will stop raining."

"Okay. But you have to go first."

So Annie begins. "When I get a dog"—pause—"her name will be Miss Phoebe!"

Then Helen. "Once I got sent to the principal's office when I forgot my homework two days in a row!"

Annie again. "Once"—pause—"I ate *eleven* cookies in a row when my father wasn't looking!"

And Helen. "I'm not allowed to walk to town without a grownup!"

Annie's eyes widen. "Yes, you are. You *told* me you're allowed."

Helen shakes her head.

"Are you sure you're not allowed?" Annie's throat begins to tighten.

"They only care about James," Helen says, "and I'm *glad* we're running away from home."

"But we're not running away," Annie whispers. Kids in books run away, not real kids—and especially not Annie. Why, she could never be a running-away-from-home kind of girl! Not really. She *likes* her home. Very much! Four hundred forty Riverside Drive, apartment 10B, is the best home in the world! And 45 Pineapple Street in the summer, that's the best home, too! She couldn't possibly run away from home! Because who will cook her dinner tonight? Or keep her company when she wakes up in the night? And how can she run away without her favorite book in the world? No sir, she would never go off—not even for a day—not without **Remembering Mrs. Rossi.** The more she thinks about it, the sadder she gets. Because while having one parent isn't nearly as good as having two, she knows she has a nice father. No, not just nice. *Very* nice. Extremely, terribly nice (even if he is a little boring sometimes), and she loves him very, very much (even if he doesn't pay attention to her sometimes), and how lonely he would be if she went away . . . *all-by-himself* lonely . . . Suddenly, Annie wants to go home. *Now.* This *second.* She is just getting up to go home, when Helen tells the saddest secret of all.

"I hope my mother never dies." When she says it, Helen starts to cry. "I hope my mother never dies." Helen says it again, and now she is sobbing loudly. This makes Annie mad. What is *she* crying for? Helen *has* a mother! Right back there on Pineapple Street! Annie is so mad—so terribly *furious,* in fact—that she starts to cry and sob, too. *Mommy, Mommy, Mommy . . . why can't you just come back? . . .*

All at once, through her tears, Annie sees her father bounding up the street: running, running, looking this way, that way, running very fast, with Al at his heels, shouting Annie's name in the rain and Helen's.

"Here I am!" Annie flies down the steps. Barefoot but fast. Way faster than Helen, and when she reaches her father, she flings herself into his arms.

"Annie. Annie." He keeps saying her name. "I've never in my *life* been so scared . . ." He is shaking and holding Annie. "The thought of losing you . . ."

"I'm sorry." Annie can barely choke out the words. She made her father scared! She made him shake! Surely, she is the most terrible child on earth!

"There, there." Meanwhile, her father has (quite sneakily) turned his attention to Helen. *Pesty old* Helen. "You're okay now," he goes on (a little too kindly). *Bratty* Helen. Why, she's the one who started all the trouble today, and everything that happened is *her* fault, not Annie's! Which Annie is just about to say . . . but then she remembers how *fast* he was running on Main Street . . . and how *sad* he was when he thought Annie was lost . . . and she changes her mind.

"Thank you for finding me, and I love you," Annie whispers. She leans against her father in the rain, wishing a hug could last forever.

The storm goes on and on, all afternoon and into the night, and Annie sets the table for an early dinner: grilled-cheese-and-tomato sandwiches. She puts the cheese on the bread and layers the cheese with slices of bright red tomato. When the sandwiches are ready for flipping, she helps her father flip.

"They can't be too dark," she warns. "They can't be too light. The cheese has to melt, but it can't dribble, or you make a big mess in the pan."

"Yes, yes, and yes."

Annie is quiet a moment, and then she says, "I'm sorry I walked to town without a grownup." Her lip quivers and she stares at her perfect sandwich. "I'm sorry I'm not perfect, and I'm sorry I made you scared, and I hope you don't wish you had another little girl instead of me for your child."

"A perfect Annie Rossi—how *boring* that would be!" Professor Rossi (as usual) laughs at his own good humor. "And as far as other little girls are concerned, forget about it, Annie. You belong to me—we belong to each other—and that's all there is to it. On the other hand," he goes on in a more serious way, "I don't know *what* you were thinking." (This is the third time, or maybe the fourth, Professor Rossi has said, "I don't know *what* you were thinking." As a rule, Annie doesn't like when he says the same thing more than one or two times, but this time she knows she has it coming.)

"I did it for Helen. To keep her company," Annie explains (again). Leaving out the other part (again). The part about whose idea it was to walk to town in the first place. "Her parents like James better," she explains (again).

"Nonsense. Her parents do *not* like James better," he says (again). "They were worried sick . . . just like me . . . and besides, a clever girl like you knows better than to go off like that, without a word to anyone."

Annie nods. She is glad her father remembers she is clever.

"Running off like that is definitely against the rules. Now and forever," he declares. "Do we understand each other, Annie?"

"Yes." Annie bites into a corner of her perfect sandwich.

"Frankly, I think we're not doing badly, you and I . . . considering . . . well, considering Mommy . . ."

"I wish Mommy could just be here," Annie says. "We *need* Mommy."

Something thumps outside on the porch. Professor Rossi opens the screen door and Al walks in. He shakes himself off.

"Hello, Al," says Professor Rossi.

Al turns his head in surprise. He opens his mouth to bark at Annie's father, but nothing comes out.

"He likes you," Annie points out. She would like to say something else, of course. *See, Daddy? I told you dogs are fun and brave. Look how SOME dogs even go out in a storm to find you!* Perhaps this isn't the day to say it, though. Tomorrow would be better—yes, tomorrow. They can walk to town, just Annie and her father. The letter from

Miss Meadows will be waiting at the post office for sure, and Annie will read it out loud, and perhaps they'll get some ice cream for the long walk home. And on the way home, she will say (in the sweetest possible way), *If we get a dog, Daddy, how about calling her Miss Phoebe?*

They have cookies on the couch for dessert, and the rain comes down over Pineapple Street. Thunder clouds roll in the skies over Pineapple Street, and Professor Rossi brings out his notebook and tells Annie something that sounds to her like a secret.

"I've been writing some things about Mommy in here."

"A *book*! Are you writing a whole *book* about Mommy?" Annie jumps off the couch. Now there will be two books about her mother!

"Well . . ." Clearing his throat. "I hardly think we can call this a book . . ."

"I hope the chapters are *short*," Annie says. "I like short chapters best, with *medium* print . . . and what about pictures? You *have* to have pictures of Mommy," she goes on. "And *me*. A picture of me with Mommy, you could put that on the cover!"

"Slow *down, Miss Boss.*" Professor Rossi whistles. "A *book* is a pretty tall order," he says. "Right now, I'm going word by word . . . day by day, trying my best to keep Mommy close . . . and let her go . . . and keep her close again . . ."

"Maybe you want someone to help you. *I* could help you. Because *I* know everything about Mommy *and* I know how to be an author."

"Interesting idea." Professor Rossi rubs his chin thoughtfully, and the sides of his face. "Of course, we'd have to keep an eye on that bossy streak of yours"—teasing—"but all things considered, Annie, I'd be *honored* to have your help."

"Really?" Breathless.

"Really."

"Good," Annie says, "and now I won't be mad at you."

"*You're* mad at *me*?"

"Yes. Because you always forget to pay attention to me, and that really hurts my feelings."

"Always?" Eyebrows up.

"Okay, *sometimes*."

"Fair enough. I will work on paying more attention to you," promises Professor Rossi. "Now, are you ready to read a few things I wrote about Mommy?"

"Wait!" Annie bolts across the room, to her pink-flowered bedroom on Pineapple Street. "I have to get something."

Remembering Mrs. Rossi is just where she'd left it this morning, under her pillow on the bed with the blue summer quilt. Annie comes back and sits right up close to her father. He reads first. Word by word from his brown notebook, and Annie loves every single word he reads about her mother. "Word by word . . .

day by day," her father had said, "trying my best to keep Mommy close . . . and let her go . . . and keep her close again." Afterward, slowly and together, they turn the pages of **Remembering Mrs. Rossi** . . . *keeping her close* . . . When they get to the end, they go back to page one and start again.

Remembering
Mrs. Rossi

by all the
great kids
in Room
222!

Shopping with Mrs. Rossi
A Poem, by Peter

Where are you, Mrs. Rossi?
Did you forget to come to school?
Where are you, Mrs. Rossi?
Don't you like us anymore?

Hey, Mrs. Rossi! I saw you
That time at the market
Yikes! Teacher in the market!
Hide! Duck! Spy!
Spy on Mrs. Rossi
Shopping with her girl
Shopping with her Annie
The way my mom shops with me

Where are you, Mrs. Rossi?
Nobody's mom should die

Some Things You Should Know about Mrs. Rossi

by Carrie

There are things you should know about
Mrs. Rossi. Like the color of her hair.
<u>Brown!</u> And guess what she eats for
lunch every day? <u>A bagel with cream
cheese and tomatoes!</u> And guess what's
on her desk? <u>Pictures of her family,
and when you look at the pictures, you
feel like you know her whole family!</u>
Mrs. Rossi is always losing her DAILY
LESSON PLANNER (10 times a day) and
guess who always finds it? <u>ME!</u> I wish I
could look inside. Just one little
second, <u>pleeeeease,</u> but no one's
allowed, not even me. Mrs. Rossi writes
top-secret stuff in there, and I bet
there's good stuff about me in there.

This is true. One time my head hurts a
little, so I get to have lunch in the
classroom. Just me and Mrs. Rossi. Then

I do something. (Shhh.) I look inside
the DAILY LESSON PLANNER. Just for a
second, but she sees. I hate how she
says, "I'm surprised at you, Carrie."
It's the second worst day of my life.

Here's the last thing you should know
about Mrs. Rossi and me and how Mrs.
Owens called my parents that day. She
told my parents and then my parents
told me, and everyone cried. Because
Mrs. Rossi died. It was the worst day
ever.

The Key and Mrs. Rossi
by Alex

One time I forgot my house key. I hate
when I forget my house key because they
don't let you go home after school.
Which isn't fair. They make you go to
the principal's office. Mrs. Owens
always says the same thing. Which is
this: I'm afraid we'll have to call
your mother at work, Alex.

I hate calling my mom at work because
her boss is mean and she has to talk in
a whisper to her own kid. When she
hears I forgot my house key again, she
gets mad because I'm never responsible
enough to suit her. Now bad news. She
can't leave work or pick me up for a
whole hour. Which isn't fair. I'm
hungry (starving) and I hate being the
last kid in school.

I sit all by myself on that hard bench
in the office and no one even talks to
me. I look in my book bag for something
to eat and there's nothing to eat, not
even gum, and if you think I'm doing
homework, forget it. Even the teachers
are going home. They're all punching
out and you never saw so many happy
teachers in your life. I say hi to Mrs.
Rossi even though I'm in a bad mood. I
tell her my mom is always late; she
needs to be more responsible. Mrs.
Rossi laughs. Which is nice because
people don't usually think I'm that
funny. Then she starts digging around
in her big bag: Cards! A box of animal
crackers, the kind little kids eat!

We play gin rummy and eat all the
crackers and I win three times. Mrs.
Rossi wins five. Then my mom comes and
I go home.

A Letter from Leo

Dear Mrs. Rossi,

I'm still pretty mad at you. I don't think you should have called my parents that time. Plus I wish you didn't call in the middle of dinner. Grownups always forget about dessert when your teacher's on the phone. Plus I wish you didn't say, LEO IS NEGLECTING HIS HOMEWORK.

Because now I'm not allowed to watch TV for the rest of my life. Plus now I have to do my homework in public every day, at the kitchen table while my mom is making dinner. Poor old Leo—work, work, work. When my dad comes home from his job at the shoe store, the whole family sits around looking at my homework. Even my little brother Herbie looks, and he can't even read! I like when my mom

says, <u>I knew you could do it, Leo.</u> I
like when my dad says, <u>Go get 'em, Leo.</u>
He always says that if you do a good
job.

Your student forever,
Leo

Birthday!

by Miriam

It is raining cats and dogs! We can't
go out for recess! Everyone's mad!
Then Mr. Rossi knocks on the door and
Mrs. Rossi jumps in the air because
here is her <u>husband</u>!! He has <u>cupcakes</u>!!
Hey, it's <u>Mrs. Rossi's birthday</u>!! We
all sing happy birthday but she won't
tell how old she is!! I love cupcakes
so much!

MRS. ROSSI WAS A SPY
by Benny

Mrs. Rossi was a spy. She had to be.
She's the only one who figured out
where I was going all those times after
school. Not even Joe figured it out,
and he's my best friend. Not even my
mom figured it out, and she's my mom.
I'm supposed to go straight home after
school. I always used to. Then I found
the firehouse. It's over on 113th
Street and I started going there. I
liked having a secret. I liked sitting
on the curb across the street from the
firehouse. I liked waiting for
something to happen. Mostly nothing
happened but that's okay. I liked
watching the guys over there when the
big red door was open. They looked
nice. I didn't say anything or wave, no
baby stuff. Sometimes I drew stuff. I'm
not a great artist or anything but I
like to draw. I guess if I keep
practicing, I'll get really good.

Then one day Mrs. Rossi the spy showed
up . . . and there goes my secret,
right out the window. Mrs. Rossi sat on
the curb. We watched the firehouse and
you could tell she liked my firehouse.
I said, My father used to be a fire-
fighter, but I think the spy already
knew. I said, He died when I was a
baby. I think she knew that, too. Then
we crossed the street. Mrs. Rossi
knocked on the big red door. We went
in. Seven is my lucky number and seven
firefighters shook my hand, and also
Mrs. Rossi's! It was the greatest day
of my life! Now when I sit on my curb,
my friends at the firehouse wave to me.
Sometimes they come over to see what
I'm drawing.

Mrs. Rossi and the Red Shoes
by Tess

Mrs. Rossi always wore plain blue shoes. One day she wore ooh-la-laaaaa fancy red shoes to school! And I saw them first, because I was the first one in school!

Me: I like your red shoes, Mrs. Rossi.

Mrs. Rossi: Thank you, Tess.

Me: Where are your regular shoes, the old blue ones?

Mrs. Rossi: Under my bed, I suppose.

Me: My mother has purple shoes. But only for special occasions. I love special occasions, Mrs. Rossi.

Mrs. Rossi: Well, then, I'll tell you a little secret. Today is a special occasion. My anniversary!

Me: Is there a party? I <u>love</u> parties, Mrs. Rossi.

Mrs. Rossi: Actually, my husband is taking me to lunch today!

Me: To a restaurant????

Mrs. Rossi: To my <u>favorite</u> restaurant. I think I'll have spaghetti.

Me: Could I come, too, Mrs. Rossi? Pleeeease! The food in this school is really bad.

This is a picture
of Mrs. Rossi
and the red shoes.
She looks pretty.
Her sweater is
red, too.

Yelena's Cheer

An Original Cheer, by Yelena

Give me an M

M!

Give me an R

R!

Give me an S

S!

Give me an R

R!

Give me an O

O!

Give me an SSI

SSI!

Who d'ya love?

Mrs. Rossi!!

Who?

Mrs. Rossi!!

One more time!

Yaaaaay, Mrs. Rossi!!

The Broken Leg
by Frankie

My name is Frankie and I feel sorry
for Mrs. Rossi. Only old people are
supposed to die. And bad guys on TV.
A lot of teachers get a headache or a
cold. Mr. Lubner the gym teacher in my
old school broke his leg that time.
I signed Frankie on his cast. I never
heard about a teacher who died. Not
even on TV. And that's why I feel
sorry for Mrs. Rossi.

The Complaint Box

by Lola

I never heard of a Complaint Box until
the first day of sixth grade and Mrs.
Rossi was telling us all about sixth
grade and Matthew said, <u>Homework on the</u>
<u>weekend?? No fair!!</u> Mrs. Rossi usually
gets mad when you call out, but that
time she said, <u>File your complaint in</u>
<u>the Complaint Box, Matthew</u>. And there
really was a box! And you're honestly
allowed to write your complaint on a
green card and drop it in the box and
you don't even have to sign your name!
I know a fancy way to say you don't
sign your name. ANONYMOUS. Sometimes
Mrs. Rossi uses big words so we all
know a few big words before the end of
sixth grade and she wrote ANONYMOUS on
the board one time and we had to write
it in our notebooks. It's my favorite
big word. Once I was mad because I
wanted to go to the park for recess

and it wasn't even raining that hard
and we had to stay in. I filed an
ANONYMOUS complaint. Once my dog stole
my assignment pad so I didn't do my
social studies homework and Mrs. Rossi
said, Under the circumstances, Lola,
you should have called a friend. She
said it in front of the whole class and
I turned red. I filed an ANONYMOUS
complaint.

Every Friday Mrs. Rossi put the
Complaint Box on her desk so she could
read all the things we wrote on green
cards. She said maybe those cards would
make her a better teacher . . . but I
think she already was the best teacher
in the world.

ANONYMOUS COMPLAINT

Mrs. Rossi forgot to say goodbye. I
really wish I could see her again.

FIGHT

by Jake

Mrs. Rossi used to get mad if you
called out and she used to get mad if
you didn't raise your hand and if you
forgot your homework and passed notes
in school and talked under your breath
and slouched. Mrs. Rossi used to get
mad if you laughed when someone messed
up and if you said something mean to a
girl and threw food in the cafeteria
and didn't empty your tray. Mrs. Rossi
used to get mad if you ran <u>up</u> the
stairs or <u>down</u> the stairs and if you
said <u>yeah</u> instead of <u>yes</u>. But watch out
if you're ever in a fight, because
that's when she got <u>really</u> mad. One
time I got in this teeny little fight
with Joe in the cafeteria (which he
started) and he got a bloody nose. Mrs.
Rossi was super-mad. Everyone went to
the nurse's office (me, Joe, Mrs.
Rossi, Mrs. Owens). Joe got to lie

down. I got to stand in a corner. Now
they're all looking at poor old Joe
with this blue ice pack on his nose. I
was hoping they'd forget about me but
no luck. Mrs. Rossi made me call Joe's
parents to explain about the teeny
little bump on his nose. She made me
call my parents, too. It was
exhausting. I was supposed to have gym
but Mrs. Rossi would not let me go to
gym. She made me stay there with Joe
until he felt better. I was mad. Then
we started fooling around. When the
nurse wasn't looking, we had a catch
with the ice pack.

Books in a Little Red Wagon

**This picture brought to you
in living color by Herman!!

**This is Mrs. Rossi's wagon. Every
week she drags it all the way to the
public library and all the way back,
just so we can have a new supply of
books in room 222. I really hate
reading. I would rather watch a scary
movie on TV. Or run around the
basketball court—it's a lot more fun
than reading.

Olivia's Confession

A True Life Story in 4 Chapters, by **Olivia**

Chapter 1: My Father and I Walk to School

My father likes walking me to school. He says walking me to school always gets his day off to a good start. We're supposed to leave the house <u>promptly at 8</u>. Sometimes we do. Sometimes we don't. Then he's late for work, I'm late for school, and no one's day is off to a good start.

Chapter 2: Two Muffins

One day we leave at 8:15. Not my fault. Halfway there, <u>uh-oh,</u> it's raining! No umbrella. Not my fault. We get a <u>little</u> wet . . . He says, <u>Poor me, soaking wet!</u> Passing Carmen's Diner—<u>mmnnn</u>—steamy hot muffins in the window.

Pleeeeease, Daddy, please!! The lady puts two in a bag. One for me, one for Mrs. Rossi (<u>That Olivia's such a nice girl</u>). I think I'll eat mine now, walking in the rain. Father says, <u>Bad idea, Olivia</u> . . . but I open the bag and pull out my beautiful muffin. Then—nooooo!!—all the rain in the world falls right on my muffin. It breaks into millions of pieces on the sidewalk. I start to cry. Father doesn't say, <u>I told you so,</u> but we both know what he's thinking.

Chapter 3: One Muffin

He drops me off at school. I am sad. I walk sadly upstairs to room 222 and I can smell Mrs. Rossi's muffin. I pick off a tiny little piece and stuff it in my mouth. I do it again . . . again . . . again . . . goodbye, muffin.

Chapter 4: Zero Muffins

Eating Mrs. Rossi's muffin wasn't the
nicest thing I've ever done in the
world. I wish I didn't do it and I'm
sorry, Mrs. Rossi. And that is my
confession.

SOFIA'S LETTER TO THE MAYOR OF NEW YORK CITY

Dear Mr. Mayor (Sir):

Did you ever hear of Mrs. Rossi? Because she used to be my teacher and she died. She wasn't even that old. Just medium old. Mrs. Rossi was extremely pretty, for a teacher. She always put on red lipstick right before lunch and she had this dressy red coat and once she let me try it on! But she didn't like spiders and one time I saw her smash a big spider. Mrs. Rossi loved books and stories and reading and one time she invited a real <u>Author</u> to our class so he could tell us how to be a famous <u>Author</u>. He was very, very old and very, very kind. He even brought slides so we could see his house and his desk and you were allowed to ask a question and I asked, <u>Do you like your</u>

job? Guess what Mrs. Rossi told the
Author? She told him we were Authors,
too!

I never met a famous Mayor before. Do
you like your job? Do you want to come
over to our school? Go to room 222.
Drew's mom made cupcakes when the
Author came over. Do you like cupcakes?
We have the best classroom. Mrs. Rossi
said it's our home away from home.
There's a science corner and library
corner and a giant map of New York
City. Mrs. Rossi made lots of red
circles around her favorite places on
the map of New York City. There's a
sign on our door. Mrs. Rossi's Class.
Nobody's allowed to touch our sign.
We're keeping it there forever.

Sincerely yours,
Sofia

Cafeteria Lady

by Sabrina

The maddest I ever saw Mrs. Rossi was
when some of the kids in the class—
okay, <u>most</u> of the kids in the class—
were mean to Mrs. Lester. That's the
lady who works in the cafeteria and I
never even knew her name was Mrs.
Lester until that day. I always just
called her the cafeteria lady.

This is what happened. It was macaroni-
and-cheese day and they started this
game. See, everyone at our table had
to say something bad about the macaroni
and cheese. I know it sounds stupid,
but if you didn't do it, they might
say something bad about you. Then Mrs.
Rossi is standing there and she makes
us go back to the classroom NO RECESS
AND NO TALKING. Not even a word. You
have to sit around and think about Mrs.

Lester's FEELINGS. And think up a way
to make Mrs. Lester feel APPRECIATED.

A lot of the kids wrote a letter of
appreciation to Mrs. Lester.
Some kids including me made a picture
of appreciation for Mrs. Lester.
Some kids wrote a poem and Julie made a
paper bracelet.
Mrs. Rossi made an invitation and we all
signed the invitation that said: <u>Please</u>
<u>come to our class tomorrow at 12:30.</u>
Tomorrow at 12:30 this is what happened.
MRS. ROSSI MADE LUNCH FOR MRS. LESTER!
She even put it on a silver platter and
Mrs. Lester even got to sit in Mrs.
Rossi's chair! We read our letters and
poems and Sofia danced. Peter even
played the trombone and Benny and Alex
sang a really crazy song and everyone
was laughing, even Benny and Alex. It
was fun and Mrs. Lester felt
appreciated.

Mrs. Rossi and Jackie Robinson and Me

by Joe

Not to brag but I'm a good (great!!) baseball player, just like Jackie Robinson. My specialty is pitching. My other specialty is hitting. I'm still not bragging but I ALWAYS get a hit. Except for that day. That Bad-Luck Saturday. Because guess who shows up in the park when I am playing baseball? Mrs. Rossi. Oh, brother. So now my teacher is watching and all I keep thinking is MY TEACHER IS WATCHING . . . MY TEACHER IS WATCHING. . . . Good-bye concentration. I strike out and strike out and strike out, and as you can see, it is all HER fault. (Mrs. Rossi's). After the game she shakes my hand. "Even Jackie Robinson didn't get a hit every time, Joe."

I wish Mrs. Rossi didn't die so she
could watch me play baseball again.
I would hit a home run, definitely.

Dear Annie Rossi,

Hi! My name is Louise! I'm in Mrs. Rossi's class. I have brown hair. Brown eyes. Next fall I'm getting braces if my mom gets big tips at the diner! I have seen your pictures on Mrs. Rossi's desk. I like the seesaw picture best. You are cute!

Very truly yours,
Louise

P.S. I wish you could be my little sister. We could share my room.

Gold Stars and Christmas Trees
by Justine

This year for my Christmas tree I'm
making a beautiful gold star for the
top of my tree in honor of Mrs. Rossi.
Whenever I look at my star, I will say
a special prayer for Mrs. Rossi.
The End.

Wait a Second, Mrs. Rossi

by Sal

I wish Mrs. Rossi would just
Show up
Come by
Hang out
Hang up her coat
Squeak chalk on the board
And yell, <u>Pay attention, Sal</u>

Wait a second, Mrs. Rossi
(I just wrote a poem)

CAN YOU BELIEVE THIS?

by Charlie

Are you ready to hear the weirdest story in the world? Are you really and truly ready? Okay. Here goes nothing.

ONCE I SAW MRS. ROSSI <u>RIDING A BIKE</u> TO SCHOOL!

It was the oldest bike you've ever seen and she locked it to a Stop Sign in front of our school.

"Hey, Mrs. Rossi!" I said. "That sure is an old bike!"

I was trying to be funny but I think I hurt her feelings. I wish I didn't hurt her feelings that time.

A Scientific Experiment

by that great scientific genius,
Matthew

<u>What You Need:</u> 1 picture of Matthew;
1 envelope; 1 balloon on a string;
strong tape; a lot of stamps

<u>Directions:</u>
1. Put picture of Matthew in envelope.
2. Print on envelope
   TO: MRS. ROSSI
   ADDRESS: HEAVEN
3. Put a lot of stamps on envelope.
4. Blow up balloon.
5. Go to Central Park. (Go ONLY on a
windy day—**<u>important</u>**.)
6. Attach envelope to balloon with
tape.
7. Count to 3. (Count SLOWLY, eyes
CLOSED—**<u>important</u>**.)

8. Let go of balloon. Open eyes. Watch balloon.
9. Keep watching balloon for a long time.

Scientific Questions:
Did the balloon get all the way to Heaven?
Did Mrs. Rossi smile when she saw the picture of Matthew?

What We Learned from Science Experiment: You can't see the balloon anymore and you can't see Mrs. Rossi, but you can remember them.

Neighbors

by Drew

My name is Drew. I live at 440
Riverside Drive. I live in apartment
1A. That's the super's house and my
father is the super. He's like the boss
of 440 and sometimes I help him fix all
the stuff that breaks such as stoves
and sinks and doorknobs. Snowy days we
shovel the sidewalk so the old people
don't fall in the snow. I love when it
snows and snows and snows and they have
to close school and I get to watch TV
and play with my puppy all day.

Okay, this is a very big secret. I know
where Mrs. Rossi lives. <u>In my building.</u>
I couldn't believe my bad luck when I
saw the 10B lady in my classroom the
first day of school. I never even knew
she was a teacher. She was just <u>that</u>
<u>lady</u> in 10B and her little kid was
always riding her bike in the lobby.

Nightmare, nightmare! What if I see my teacher in the laundry room doing laundry! Nightmare, nightmare! What if she comes to my <u>house</u> and tells my parents all the things I do wrong in school! Nightmare, nightmare! What if the kids in my class find out . . . and everyone calls me teacher's pet! I kept waiting for Mrs. Rossi to tell the secret. She never told. Which was nice of Mrs. Rossi.

Yesterday after school I took the elevator to the tenth floor and looked at the door that said 10B. I was sad because <u>that lady</u> doesn't live there anymore.

Memo to: Mr. Shaw (the Sub)

From: Julie

If you tell me one more time
Write a few words about Mrs. Rossi
I will scream
Or
I might report you
To my
Tall
Father
(He always takes my side)
Or
I might say
Fine, Mr. Shaw, here you are, Mr. Sub
And here come the words
MRS. ROSSI HAD A RED DRESS

If you tell me one more time
Write a bit more, Julie
I will
Scream
Or
I might say

Fine, Mr. Shaw, here you are, Mr. Sub
And here come the words
MRS. ROSSI HAD A RED DRESS
MY MOTHER HAD A RED DRESS
MY MOTHER LEFT HER RED DRESS
IN THE CLOSET AND LEFT
And by the way, Mr. Shaw, by the way,
 Mr. Sub . . .
ALL RED DRESSES MAKE ME SAD

Bossy Mrs. Rossi
A Love Poem, by Liliana

Pay attention
No talking!
Neat homework
No pushing!
Notebooks out
No slouching!
Spelling counts
No running!
Math test
No cheating!
Pencils down
No groaning!
Raise hands
No whining!
Pay attention
I love this class
We love you, too, Mrs. Rossi!